Book 3: Hijack

Also by Chris Bradford

The Bodyguard series
Book 1: Recruit
Book 2: Hostage
Book 3: Hijack
Book 4: Ransom

Book 3: Hijack

Chris Bradford

Philomel Books

For my godparents, Ann and Andrew:

Thanks for looking out for me all my life.

PHILOMEL BOOKS
an imprint of Penguin Random House LLC
375 Hudson Street, New York, NY 10014

Library of Congress Cataloging-in-Publication Data is available upon request.
Printed in the United States of America.
ISBN 9781524737016
10 9 8 7 6 5 4 3 2 1

American edition edited by Brian Geffen.
American edition design by Jennifer Chung.
Text set in 11-point Palatino Nova.

"The best bodyguard is the one nobody notices."

With the rise of teen stars, the intense media focus on celebrity families and a new wave of millionaires and billionaires, adults are no longer the only target for hostage-taking, blackmail and assassination—kids are too.

That's why they need specialized protection . . .

GUARDIAN

Guardian is a secret close-protection organization that differs from all other security outfits by training and supplying only young bodyguards.

Known as guardians, these highly skilled kids are more effective than the typical adult bodyguard, who can easily draw unwanted attention. Operating invisibly as a child's constant companion, a guardian provides the greatest possible protection for any high-profile or vulnerable young target.

In a life-threatening situation, a **guardian** is the final ring of defense.

PREVIOUSLY ON BODYGUARD . . .

"Bodyguards are the modern-day samurai warriors," declared Colonel Black, clicking up an image of a Japanese swordsman on the overhead projector. "Like these ancient warriors, the bodyguard's duty is to protect their Principal above all else."

——— ———

To fulfill that duty, new Guardian recruit Connor Reeves gets a crash course in unarmed combat . . .

"Have you heard of Bruce Lee's one-inch punch?"

Connor nodded.

"Well, this is the one-inch push."

With barely more than a flick of his wrist, Steve palmed Connor in the chest. Taken completely by surprise, Connor staggered backward and then collapsed to the floor, gasping for breath. A concussive wave of pain spread through his lungs, and his chest felt as if it had imploded.

"Effective, isn't it?"

——— ———

**After only ten weeks of training, Connor is shocked to
be assigned his first mission—to protect Alicia Mendez,
the US president's daughter . . .**

Marc whistled through his teeth in awe. "Better you than
me, Connor."

"Yeah," agreed Ling. "You're going in at the deep end!"

Connor thought there had to be some sort of mistake.
"They're right, Colonel. I haven't even done a test operation
yet."

The colonel looked him in the eye. "I won't lie to you,
Connor. This is the highest-profile assignment the Guardian
has ever been involved in. For us, we're taking a huge gam-
ble. For you, it will be a baptism of fire."

———

**But Connor's mission is complicated by an impulsive
Principal . . .**

"Care to join me on a little adventure?" whispered Alicia,
a mischievous grin on her face.

"What do you mean?" asked Connor.

Alicia glanced toward an emergency exit at the back of
the store.

Immediately grasping her intentions, Connor replied, "I
don't think that's a good idea."

"Oh, don't be such a killjoy! Even a soldier's son must

have broken the rules."

"Your father wouldn't be happy."

"I don't *care* what he thinks," she shot back. "Besides, what's the worst that could happen?"

———

Little does Alicia know that a terrorist sleeper cell has been activated, its mission to take the president's daughter hostage . . .

"Eagle Chick has taken the bait."

"All according to plan, then," said Malik. "And you're certain her messages have been blocked?"

Bahir nodded with a self-satisfied grin.

"Good work, Bahir. You certainly excelled in the task I set."

He looked over at Hazim in the driver's seat. "And well done, Hazim, for planting the bug in the first place."

Hazim managed an anxious smile as Bahir announced, "Target is five minutes out."

———

But the terrorists didn't plan for Connor Reeves as her guardian . . .

"We'll never make it."

"Imagine you're at a track meet racing to the finish line," said Connor.

Alicia managed a strained smile. "Okay, but I'm usually not shot at!"

She took a deep breath and steeled herself for the perilous sprint.

"On your mark," said the driver. "Three . . . two . . ."

Gripping the handle of his backpack, Connor prayed the liquid body armor would do its job.

". . . one . . . GO!"

———

And when the stakes become life or death, Connor is determined to protect Alicia . . . no matter the cost . . .

Connor sensed the tight knot of terror in Alicia's heart at being left to cope on her own.

"I won't leave you," he said.

"But you might not have a choice."

Connor held Alicia close. "I made a promise to your father that I'd protect you, just like my father protected yours. And I will . . . on my life."

Now Connor embarks on his second thrilling assignment . . .

PROLOGUE

The girl felt the cold hard barrel of a gun thrust against the back of her head.

"Kneel," ordered the man, his voice as dry and cruel as the desert wind.

With no choice but to obey, the girl blindly sought the floor. The dusty rag around her eyes let in only glimpses of light, its fraying cloth reeking of stale sweat. She winced as the dirt floor grazed her bare knees and drew blood. Then, hearing the ominous *click* of a round entering the gun's chamber, her body instinctively stiffened.

Her captor leaned in close. His breath, a bitter mix of coffee and nicotine, was warm and familiar in her ear. "Farewell, my little sparrow."

So this is it, she thought with a numbness born out of exhaustion. After weeks of uncertainty and too many sleepless nights to count, she was beyond caring. Beyond even fear. In truth, her heart almost welcomed the end to her ordeal.

But, as she waited for the inevitable bullet, a small voice of fury rose within her.

Why have I been abandoned like this? Why hasn't the ransom been paid? What's gone wrong?

Despite all the promises and hopes she'd clung to, she was going to die. A bullet through the head. Her body dumped in the desert.

"Get it over with," she muttered, willing her executioner to pull the trigger and end her suffering.

Silence.

No click. No bang. Not even a reply. Only the buzz of flies circling in the stifling heat.

What's taking him so long? Is this another one of his mind games?

A bead of sweat rolled from beneath her blindfold and down her grime-covered cheek.

"Lost your nerve, have you?" she croaked, her voice quavering as her impatience turned to frustrated anger. Still no answer.

With a trembling hand, she removed the rag. Blinking away the dust, she discovered she was *alone* . . . abandoned in the center of a single-room mud-brick building. A makeshift wooden door barred the only entrance through which beams of sunlight speared the darkness.

Should I try to escape? But she had no idea what lay beyond the doorway. Her captor? The barrel of a gun? Most likely miles of unbroken desert—

Suddenly the door burst open and she was dazzled by the glaring African sun. A shadow passed across her face as a huge man filled the doorway. Dressed in khaki army fatigues and his finger primed on the trigger of an assault rifle, he swiftly scanned the room for threats before his gaze targeted her.

"Emily Sterling?" the soldier grunted.

Her throat too dry to reply, Emily managed a weak nod.

The soldier thumbed his radio mic. "Yankee Four to X-ray, hostage found alive, I repeat, *alive.*"

Scooping Emily up in his arms like a fragile doll, the soldier carried her to the door.

As the realization of her rescue hit her, Emily began to sob uncontrollably.

"It's over," promised the soldier. "You're safe now."

No, thought Emily as her tears dripped onto the man's shirt. *I'll never be safe again.*

1

"Keep your head down!" Connor shouted as a barrage of bullets raked the brick wall.

His Principal had gone into shock and kept trying to bolt from their hiding place. But that was the worst possible reaction the boy could have. A casual stroll down the street had turned into a bodyguard's nightmare, and now they were pinned down in a well-planned ambush.

Connor knew his next move would be crucial. In his head, he ran through the A-C-E procedure . . .

Assess the threat. Two shooters. One in an alley. Another behind a tree. Intention to kill, not capture.

Counter the danger. His first priority was to find cover and secure the Principal. But the low brick wall they had hidden behind provided only temporary protection. As soon as the shooters repositioned themselves, he and his Principal would be exposed again.

Escape the kill zone. Easier said than done!

4

Connor tapped his mic. "Alpha One to Control. Request emergency EVAC."

His earpiece burst into life and he heard Charley, Alpha team's operations leader, respond, *"Alpha One, this is Control. Backup on its way. Three minutes out."*

Three minutes? thought Connor. They'd be dead meat in that time. And, without any firepower of their own, they were defenseless. Connor needed an exit strategy . . . and fast.

Covering the Principal with his body, Connor peeked over the wall and scanned the immediate area. A clump of bushes off to their right gave some visual cover for an escape but no physical protection from gunfire. A car parked farther down the street provided little hope; he was too young to know how to drive, let alone how to hot-wire a car! He looked at the building behind them—a small warehouse with offices attached. The back entrance was only thirty feet away, but it was across open ground. Checking on the enemy's progress, Connor saw that the shooter behind the tree was advancing to get a clear shot. He had no choice but to risk it.

"Move!" he growled, seizing his Principal by the arm and sprinting toward the warehouse.

Keeping his body close, Connor shielded the boy as the enemy opened fire. Bullets whizzed past. One almost clipped his ear. Their feet pounded across the pavement, and whether through speed or pure luck, they made it to the entrance unharmed.

Connor yanked on the handle.

"NO!" he cried, tugging furiously at the locked doors.

He spun around. They were now sitting ducks. Connor shoved his Principal into the shelter of a large wheeled Dumpster. The boy tried to run on, crying, "I don't want to die!"

"Stay down," Connor ordered, pushing him to the ground. Then through clenched teeth he added, "Amir, you're not making this any easier for me."

"Sorry," replied his friend, offering a flash of a grin from behind his safety goggles. "But I'm supposed to be a panicking Principal."

"Well, panic *less*," Connor pleaded as several bullets thudded into the metal bin.

Amir flinched and covered his head with his arms. "A bit difficult under the circumstances, don't you think?"

Richie, who was playing the part of the first shooter in the training scenario, had left his position in the alley and was unleashing a hail of paintballs from his assault rifle. So was Ling, the other shooter, who by now had reached the far end of the low wall. If either of them managed to hit Amir with even a single paintball, Connor would instantly fail the exercise.

Ever since his successful assignment protecting the American president's daughter the month before, the rest of Alpha team had been impressed but also a little envious of his newly acquired status. The only other person on the team to have earned a gold Guardian badge was Charley—and she truly deserved it, whereas he was just a first-time rookie.

That's why certain fellow guardians had made it their mission to test him to the limit—in Ling's words, "to make sure Connor doesn't get too big for his britches." Although Connor had no problem with a bit of good-natured teasing, deep down he questioned whether his first assignment had just been beginner's luck. It was true his father had been in the Special Air Service, a unit of the British Special Forces, and been one of the best bodyguards on the circuit. But that didn't mean Connor was made of the same stuff. For his own peace of mind, he needed to prove himself . . . beyond a doubt.

Connor clicked his mic again. "Alpha One to Control. Where's my pickup?"

"Alpha One. Thirty seconds out. Maintain position."

As more paintballs thudded into the bin and splattered the pavement at their feet, Connor wondered, *Do I have any other choice?*

Richie closed in, setting his sights on Amir. Connor pressed Amir farther down behind the Dumpster. Paintballs rattled off it like hailstones. A black 4×4 Range Rover roared down the road, its tires screeching as the driver braked hard and spun the armored vehicle to form a shield against

Richie's attack. The paintballs now pinged harmlessly off the bodywork.

But that still left Ling as a threat. With fifteen meters of open ground between them, she *couldn't* miss her target. Connor realized he was in a no-win situation. Whether they ran or stayed put, one or both of them would be shot down.

Then Connor had an idea. Kicking off the Dumpster's brakes, he grabbed Amir and shoved the huge container with his shoulder.

"What on earth are you doing?" cried Amir as the wheeled Dumpster began rolling down the path toward the Range Rover and Connor pushed him ahead to stay covered.

"Getting rid of the garbage," replied Connor with a grin as the Dumpster resounded with the furious impact of Ling's paintballs. The Dumpster was picking up speed now, and Connor and Amir had to sprint alongside it to stay shielded from Ling's assault. Then the Dumpster struck the wall and came to a dead stop. Having lost their only cover, the two of them made a final mad dash for the Range Rover.

Paintballs peppered the hood and windshield as Connor wrenched the back door open and shoved Amir inside. Connor dived in after him, landing on top of him in the footwell.

"GO! GO! GO!" he screamed at the driver.

Flooring the accelerator, the driver sped away from the kill zone.

2

Connor allowed himself a quiet smile of satisfaction. Against all the odds, he'd done it. He'd saved his Principal. Then Amir turned to him, and the smile was wiped from his face. Planted squarely in the right eye of Amir's goggles was the red *splat* of an exploded paintball.

"How come you got hit?" Connor exclaimed, clambering into the passenger seat and thumping the armrest in frustration. "I had you covered on all sides."

Amir tenderly peeled off his safety goggles and rubbed the bridge of his nose. Originally from Delhi, Amir was a slender boy with an angular face, bright eyes and a slick of black hair. "I wish you *had* protected me. That really hurt."

The driver brought the Range Rover to a halt and glanced over her shoulder at them. Jody, a former SO14 royal protection officer, was one of their instructors at the Guardian Training Headquarters in Wales. Kitted out in a black-and-red tracksuit, her dark brown hair bunched in a ponytail, she looked more like a personal fitness trainer than a body-guard. But that was the point. Few people ever suspected women to be part of a close-protection team, and that gave them an edge.

"Exercise over, Connor—your Principal's definitely dead," she said, arching a slim eyebrow in amusement at Amir's paint-splattered face. Then her expression hardened. "If that had been a soft-nosed sniper bullet, Amir would be headless now."

"That wouldn't be such a bad thing," remarked Charley, who sat in the front passenger seat. "He doesn't use it much anyway," she added in her sun-soaked Californian tones, shooting him a wink.

Amir's mouth fell open in exaggerated offense. "Hey! *You* can be the Principal next time."

Staring out of the passenger window, Charley sighed to herself. "If only . . ."

As Jody spun the Range Rover around, Connor caught sight of Charley's reflection in the glass. Her sky-blue eyes had lost their sparkle, and her usual confidence appeared to have faltered for a moment.

"Nothing to keep you from being the shooter next time," Connor suggested.

In the window, he saw Charley brush aside a loose strand of blond hair as her smile returned.

"That would be unfair," she replied, her reflected eyes

meeting his and narrowing in challenge. "You wouldn't last ten seconds."

Connor laughed. He didn't doubt it. Despite the difficulties she faced, Charley was a girl of many talents: a former Quiksilver Junior Surfing Champion, she was also a skillful martial artist as well as fluent in Mandarin. For all Connor knew, she was probably an elite markswoman too.

Jody parked in front of the abandoned warehouse and ordered Connor and Amir out as the other members of Alpha team gathered for the training debrief. Marc, a lean boy with bleached-blond hair who'd been filming the training exercise for class assessment, patted Connor sympathetically on the back. "*Quelle malchance!* You were almost home free."

Opening the door for Charley, Connor shrugged at his French friend. "Yep, almost."

"*Almost* is no good for a bodyguard," Ling pointed out, hefting a gun that looked huge against her tiny, sleek figure. Her oval face was framed by a bob of jet-black hair, and a silver piercing glinted on one side of her elfin nose.

"Yeah," Richie agreed in his thick Irish accent. "It's like *almost* jumping out of the way of a train. You still get hit." He fired off a couple of paintballs at the abandoned Dumpster for effect.

"*Cease fire!*" scolded Jody as she took Charley's wheelchair out of the back of the Range Rover. "Not everyone's wearing safety goggles."

"Sorry, miss," Richie replied. He offered an apologetic grin, his braces catching the sunlight like a diamond-toothed rapper. "Just celebrating our victory."

Charley slid nimbly into her chair and joined the rest of them. But Connor noticed there was still one person missing from the team.

"Bull's-eye!" shouted Jason, suddenly dropping down from the fire escape of the building opposite. He strode over with his paintball gun slung across his shoulder like Rambo. He was muscular for his age, with a thickset jaw and tousled dark hair, and Connor wouldn't have been surprised if his Aussie teammate had actually thought he *was* Rambo.

"I should change sides and become an assassin," said Jason, high-fiving Richie and Ling.

"You kill me," cooed Ling, her half-moon eyes twinkling mischievously as she dead-punched him on the arm in return. "Or at least . . . you could try."

"You were on the *roof*?" challenged Connor. "I thought there were only two shooters in this exercise."

Jason shrugged. "Sorry to disappoint you."

"But that's unfair," said Connor, turning to Jody for an explanation. "Everyone else had just two."

"As a bodyguard, you can't presume anything," she replied. "Threats can come from all directions and there can be any number of them. That's why you need to have eyes in the back of your head."

She addressed the rest of Alpha team. "Under the stress of a combat situation, your body floods with adrenaline and stress hormones. Although this benefits your strength and ability to react, one of the negative effects is 'tunnel vision.' You lose your peripheral sight and focus only on the danger in front of you. As Connor's just experienced, that can lead to fatal mistakes."

Connor gave a dismayed sigh. He hadn't looked up once during the exercise. This was his *fourth* failed test in a row. Given his poor performance, he was seriously beginning to question his abilities as a bodyguard.

"Don't look so glum," said Marc. "The Dumpster was a clever idea. I got it all on video. It was hilarious!"

"And effective," Ling admitted grudgingly. "I wasted all my ammo trying to hit you."

"But the Dumpster wouldn't have protected them from real bullets," Jason was quick to point out.

"An unseen target is harder to hit," countered Charley. "It was a good distraction."

Jody nodded in agreement. "That's very true. Connor's tactic would have increased their chances of survival. However"— she pointed to the paint-smeared Range Rover—"since he didn't protect his Principal, it's his job to clean the car."

3

"Mr. Gibb! Mr. Gibb! Are these accusations true?"

"No comment," mumbled the Australian minister for resources and energy as he fought his way through the pack of reporters. A camera was thrust into his haggard face, its flash half blinding him. He angrily pushed it away.

"Do you intend to resign?" shouted another reporter.

"How much money did you make from the deal?"

"No comment," spat Harry Gibb, reaching the glass doors and squeezing through to the air-conditioned safety of the Canberra governmental building. The security guards kept the press pack at bay as Harry scuttled across the polished marble floor toward the elevator. He jabbed a pudgy finger at the Call button, and a moment later a *ping* signaled the doors sliding open.

"Harry!" called a familiar voice from behind him.

The senator's tone was sharp. But Harry, pretending not to have heard his colleague, entered the elevator and thumbed the Close-Doors button. The senator increased his pace but was a second too late, and the metal doors clanged shut in his face.

As the elevator rose steadily, Harry took the brief moment of peace to slick down his thinning windswept hair and adjust his tie. He was breathless and could feel patches of sweat seeping through his shirt. At the fifth floor he exited. A potbellied man whose suits always failed to fit him, Harry strode through the open-plan office with as much dignity and authority as he could muster. He knew everyone would have heard the news by now. He was a marked man. But he refused to show it.

As he approached his own office, his secretary rose to greet him. She sheepishly offered him that day's mail, but he dismissed it with an irritated wave of his hand.

"Later," he muttered, conscious of the uncomfortable silence that had descended over the workplace.

Shutting his office door behind him, he dropped his briefcase and slumped into his high-backed leather chair. Rubbing his bloodshot eyes, he let out a troubled sigh. For a moment, he allowed himself to believe that he'd escaped the political storm threatening to engulf him. Then, on opening his eyes, he was confronted by an edition of the *Australian Daily* on his desk. His hangdog face was plastered across the front page. The headline ran:

MINISTER FOR MINES LINES HIS OWN POCKETS WITH GOLD

Harry glared at the offending words, a vein throbbing in his temple.

His phone rang, demanding his attention. He ignored it.

As he stared at the accusing newspaper, Harry suddenly felt his chest tighten. He scrabbled in his desk drawer for his bottle of heart pills. He shook several of the beta-blocker tablets into his open palm and dry-swallowed them.

Leaning back in his chair, Harry waited for his chest pain to pass. As the angina slowly subsided, his anger began to rise again.

"That interfering snake!" he snarled, slamming his palm on the mahogany desk and sending the newspaper flying across the floor.

His mind swirled with furious thoughts. Just because Sterling owned the *Australian Daily* and virtually every other national newspaper, that didn't give him the right to meddle in his affairs. It wasn't as if the media magnate's hands were squeaky clean. How many times had that slippery fish managed to escape prosecution for tax avoidance, illegal takeovers and business scandals? Sterling was at least as corrupt as he was, if not more so!

Harry was a *victim* of Sterling's need for scandalous head-lines. The target of an overzealous smear campaign simply to sell more newspapers. But Harry Gibb hadn't gotten this far in politics without knowing how to protect his own interests. And he certainly wouldn't roll over and die without a fight.

He was a survivor. He would do *whatever* it took to save himself.

4

The sun shone brightly. The crowd cheered. American flags and pennants fluttered wildly. Connor stood at the edge of the podium scanning the joyous faces as the US president delivered his speech. "I prayed for a miracle, and one was delivered . . ."

The western end of the National Mall was overflowing with the smiling faces of men, women and children, all gathered to celebrate the president's daughter's safe return.

But Connor wasn't celebrating. He was looking for a face. The face of a killer.

It was like searching for a hornet in a hive of bees. The assassin would blend in, become the gray person in the crowd. And that made everyone a potential suspect . . . Then Connor's eyes homed in on the barrel of a gun, protruding between a boy and his younger sister. The president beckoned for his daughter, Alicia, to join him. The gun sights tracked her as she stepped onto the stage. The siblings continued to flourish their flags, oblivious to the lethal weapon between them. Connor screamed at the Secret Service agents stationed by the barrier. But none heard him above the roar of the crowd.

In desperation Connor rushed onto the stage. But gravity seemed to weigh him down. The harder he ran, the more slowly he went. He cried out a warning. Turning, Alicia gave him a bemused look.

A noise as loud as a thunder crack punctured the cheers. Connor thought he could see the actual bullet emerge from the gun barrel. He dived into its line of fire. But the deadly bullet whizzed past, missing him by a fraction of an inch. He landed in a useless heap on the stage as Alicia gazed down in shock at the bloodred stain blossoming over her crisp white dress.

"NO!" cried Connor, watching her crumple slowly to the ground . . .

"Connor! Connor! Are you all right?"

Shaken by the shoulder, Connor blinked, disoriented for a moment. The room was swallowed in darkness, just a rectangle of muted light spilling across his bedroom floor from the open doorway.

"You were crying out," said Charley, who sat beside his bed in her wheelchair, her face half in shadow. She took her hand away from his shoulder. "I hope you don't mind me checking on you."

Connor sat up and rubbed his eyes. "No . . . not at all . . . I was just dreaming."

"Sounded more like a nightmare to me."

Connor hesitated, unsure whether admitting his inner doubts would be regarded as weakness for a guardian. Then he realized that of all the members of Alpha team, Charley would be the one to understand most.

"I keep reliving Alicia's assassination attempt."

"Near-death experiences can do that to you." A haunted look entered her eyes but was gone so quickly that Connor could have been mistaken.

"But in my dream I'm always *too late*," he explained.

"It was a close call. You got shot. So such anxiety is understandable. But you *did* save her."

"I know, but what if that was just beginner's luck? I mean, I've not passed a single Guardian training exercise this last week."

"Training is where you're supposed to make your mistakes," she reminded him. "Besides, the tests are designed to be tough so that we're at the top of our game when we're on an assignment."

Connor let out a weary sigh. He felt the mounting pressure of his forthcoming mission. The responsibility of protecting another person was overwhelming. "But what if next time I don't react quickly enough?"

Charley gave him a disapproving look. "You mustn't allow

yourself to think like that. You *did* protect the president's daughter when the time came. That should be proof enough that you're up to the job."

"Exactly my point. Everyone thinks I'm this hotshot bodyguard. But I'm not. A second later and . . ." His voice faded into silence at the terrible thought.

Charley glanced toward his bedside table, where a plastic key fob was propped up against his alarm clock. "Listen, it's in your blood, remember?" she said softly, nodding toward the key fob.

Connor studied the faded photo beneath its scratched surface. His late father, Justin Reeves, stared back at him. Tanned, tough and with the piercing green-blue eyes that Connor had inherited, his father looked every inch the soldier—a man who could be relied upon in even the most dangerous situations.

Connor felt a weight even heavier than responsibility upon his shoulders. "I'm *not* my father," he admitted quietly. "As much as Colonel Black believes I am, I can't live up to his name. Dad was Special Forces. I'm Special *Nothing*."

Charley's eyes met his with a fierce intensity. "That's negative thinking. Of course you're going to fail if that's your attitude! Listen to me. You can't measure yourself against a memory."

Connor was taken aback by her sudden fire. "I know. You're right. It's just—"

A door creaked open somewhere down the hallway. They weren't supposed to be in each other's rooms after ten o'clock at night. Charley eased herself back toward the door. At the threshold, she paused and looked at him.

"Don't doubt yourself, Connor. Whenever I question my own abilities, I remember the saying *Whether you think you can or think you can't, you're probably right.*"

She shut the door and Connor lay in the darkness, thinking about what she had said. About the power of self-belief. As he closed his eyes, he pictured his father's face willing him on, like he always had when he was alive.

5

"Operation Gemini commences in two weeks," announced Colonel Black. "I trust you've all done your homework."

The colonel stood, arms behind his back, at the front of Alpha team's briefing room. His broad shoulders, chiseled jaw and silver-gray crew cut were highlighted by the glow of the projector screen. As founder and commander of the Guardian organization, the ex-SAS soldier took a personal interest in every assignment and made certain he attended every operational briefing. On the screen behind him, spinning in 3-D, was Guardian's official logo: a silver winged shield.

Connor swiped a finger across his new tablet computer and prepared to take notes. The next few hours would be an onslaught of information from each Alpha team member about different aspects of the operation: Principal profile, location intel, threat assessments, security requirements, "action-on" procedures, role assignment and logistical support, to name but a few. Each element was crucial to the success of the mission, and all team members were required to have a working knowledge in case of role swaps or last-minute replacements.

Colonel Black stepped aside to allow Charley to the front. As Alpha team's operations leader and most experienced guardian, she always led the briefing.

"On this assignment, there are *two* Principals needing our protection," she explained, clicking the projector's handheld remote. A photograph of two young girls, virtually identical, flashed up on the screen. "These are the twin daughters of Mr. Maddox Sterling, the Australian media mogul and billionaire."

"They look like the Valley Sisters," cracked Richie with an approving grin, referring to the famous teenage TV pop duo.

"I bet you have all of their albums!" teased Ling.

"No! Of course not. I have musical taste . . . unlike you. I mean, Black Sabbath. Talk about morbid."

Ling narrowed her eyes at him. "You haven't *lived* until you've listened to *Paranoid*."

Tuning out his teammates' bickering, Connor carefully studied the photograph. The young twins had matching straw-blond hair, sea-green eyes and well-defined cheek-bones. They could very easily pass as pop stars—and equally as each other. It would be hard to tell them apart.

Pointing to the girl on the right, Charley continued with

the Principal profile. "Chloe is the eldest by twelve minutes. She's outgoing, sociable and intelligent, though word has it, she can be a bit of a princess." Charley shrugged as if to imply that that came with being the daughter of a billionaire. "Emily, on the other hand, is quieter and more introverted. She enjoys reading, nature and walking, in contrast to Chloe's love of volleyball and sunbathing. But that isn't surprising. Last year she was the victim of a kidnapping."

"Sounds like they hired us too late," quipped Amir, looking around at the others to join in his joke.

However, a stern glance from the colonel's flint-gray eyes swiftly ended Amir's attempt at humor. "Tragically, that's often the case. Hindsight brings wisdom."

On the screen, Charley flicked to a composite image of various newspaper clippings. Bullet points in front of the headlines traced the distressing progress of the kidnapping: STERLING GIRL MISSING . . . HAVE YOU SEEN EMILY? . . . MEDIA MOGUL'S MULTIMILLION-DOLLAR RANSOM DEMAND . . . HOSTAGE GIRL NEGOTIATIONS STALL . . . IS EMILY DEAD? . . . STERLING SISTER RELEASED.

"Emily was snatched while on a family vacation in the Côte d'Azur," Charley explained. "The Corsican Mafia was the suspected organization behind the kidnapping, although that wasn't proved. She was held in the Algerian desert for several months before eventually being released after lengthy negotiations over the ransom payment."

Ling held up a hand to ask a question. "If the father's so wealthy, what took so long?"

Colonel Black replied, "Ransom negotiations are rarely straightforward. There's a great deal of bluff and counter-bluff, rejected offers and impossible demands. The most important thing is that the hostage was released, unharmed."

"So, how's Emily doing now?" asked Connor.

"Surprisingly well," Charley revealed, pulling a medical report from her file. "Physically she is fit and healthy, with no lasting aftereffects. Her psychological report from her therapist, though, indicates occasional mood swings, withdrawal and a fear of the dark and confined spaces. Emily's been prescribed medication to help her cope with the anxiety attacks—but it can have side effects of drowsiness, confusion and impaired thinking. However, that's all to be expected, considering her ordeal. Alpha team's task is to ensure that such a tragedy doesn't happen again."

Clicking her remote, Charley pulled up a map of the Indian Ocean. "We will provide low-profile protection for the Sterling sisters during their upcoming vacation in the Seychelles and the Maldives." She indicated the two tiny clusters of tropical islands amid the vast blue swath of ocean separating Africa and India. "The operation will last a month and be based on Mr. Sterling's yacht."

A sleek one-hundred-and-fifty-foot multidecked super-yacht filled the display.

"Wow!" exclaimed Amir, his coffee-brown eyes widening in amazement. "That's some boat."

"That's no boat; it's a floating palace," Marc corrected as he squinted at the yacht's top deck. "It's even got a *hot tub*."

Jason shot Connor an envious glance. "You've landed a cushy assignment," he said. "Must be your reward for saving the president's daughter."

"You think so?" replied Connor, recalling the difficulties he'd faced protecting just one Principal. "I figure twins mean twice the trouble."

6

"You have to be careful with female Principals, don't you, Connor?" said Charley, glancing meaningfully in his direction.

Her comment went over the heads of the others, but Connor knew Charley was referring to the time she'd caught him and Alicia kissing. As a guardian, he knew that was a line never to be crossed—although strictly speaking, he'd no longer been protecting Alicia at that intimate moment. But Charley clearly wasn't going to let him forget it.

"And for that reason," Charley continued, ignoring the team's bemused expressions, "Colonel Black has decided there'll be *two* guardians on this operation."

The room went quiet as this new information sank in. No one had anticipated the need for a *second* operative. Yet, with two Principals to look after, having a dual protection unit was logical for effective security.

All eyes turned to the colonel. Jason straightened himself in expectation. Marc, in inverse proportion to his eagerness, leaned back casually in his chair. Ling tensely bit her lower lip, and Amir was so on the edge of his seat that he was in danger of falling off. Richie simply chewed on a fingernail, aware that he was out of the running, having only just returned from an assignment. As much as Connor respected the others on his team, he hoped the colonel would select Amir. He knew his friend was desperate to go on his first assignment and earn his winged badge.

Colonel Black held them in suspense for only a few seconds. "Ling, you'll be guardian two i/c."

"Yes!" said Ling, clenching her fist in delight.

Jason bumped fists with Ling in respect. "Congratulations, Captain. Best get your bikini ready."

"Oh, and I thought I could borrow *yours*," she said, winking at him playfully.

Meanwhile, Amir quietly deflated like a punctured balloon.

Connor offered his friend an encouraging smile. "Don't worry, there's always next time," he whispered.

Amir gave a halfhearted nod by way of reply.

But as the colonel's exact words registered with Ling, her delight turned to a frown. "Two i/c? *Second* in charge?"

The colonel raised an eyebrow. "You have a problem with that?"

"Of course not," said Ling, offering an amiable smile at Connor. "It's just that this being my third mission, I thought—"

"You'll both have *equal* responsibilities when it comes to protecting your Principals," cut in the colonel. "But there must always be a clear chain of command on the ground. Now, Amir, brief the team on the threat situation ... Amir?"

Amir looked up. Rousing himself from his disheartened daze, he headed over to the lectern and busied himself connecting his tablet to the projector, taking a little longer than necessary in an attempt to hide his disappointment. Clearing his throat, he began to read directly from his notes, barely glancing up.

"I'll start with the Principals' father: Maddox Sterling. Fifty years old, he's the founder and chairman of Fourth Estate Corporation, Australia's largest media company."

A suave silver-haired man in a well-cut suit appeared on the screen.

"The corporation's interests include newspaper and magazine publishing, Internet, cable TV, and film and television production. Fourth Estate essentially owns and controls Australia's national media."

Amir clicked through a series of images showing various newspapers, movie posters and TV channels.

"Because of this, Mr. Sterling has many powerful allies in both government and industry. Equally he has made many enemies—as a result of his aggressive business tactics or his newspapers' controversial style of investigative journalism.

For example"—a slide of a slim, dark-haired woman popped up—"the former government opposition leader Kelly Brocker was forced to resign last year after revelations about her private life."

Amir switched to an image of a tanned middle-aged man with auburn hair. "This is Joseph Ward, the former CEO of Ward Enterprises, who was jailed for ten years for corporate fraud. The financial scandal was exposed by *Insider*, a true crime show on one of Mr. Sterling's TV networks. As a result, Mr. Ward, a business rival of Mr. Sterling, has declared bankruptcy, and the media arm of his company was absorbed by none other than Fourth Estate." Amir raised his eyebrows at the significance of this coincidence. "At the time of his arrest, Mr. Ward publicly vowed revenge on Mr. Sterling, although currently Mr. Ward remains in jail.

"Then the most recent case is the exposure of a high-level Australian politician, Harry Gibb, who has been accused of financial misconduct over the country's mining rights."

A front page from the *Australian Daily* flashed up, the headline declaring, GREEDY GIBB MUST GO! This statement was supported by an unflattering photo of a portly gentleman with thinning hair and a ruddy complexion, caught at the moment he was stuffing a large burger into his mouth.

"Although none of these people are a direct threat to our two Principals," explained Amir, "any enemy of the father must be considered a potential enemy of the daughters. So I've included full background intel on each of them in your operation folders."

"What about their mother?" asked Ling. "What's her story?"

"Sadly," said Amir, "the mother died in a car crash when the girls were only eight years old."

Connor felt his throat tighten at the news. Having lost his father around the same age, he could understand what life must be like for the girls.

"Recently, however, their father got engaged." Amir pressed the remote a few times to bring up a picture of the new fiancée: a glamorous and unexpectedly youthful woman in a figure-hugging red dress. "Amanda Ryder is a twenty-nine-year-old swimsuit model who is a regular on the Sydney socialite circuit. As a future member of the family, she'll be joining you on the yacht."

"Should make for an *entertaining* vacation," said Marc, with a sly grin at Connor.

Connor stifled a snigger at his friend's remark.

"Boys, focus on the mission!" snapped Colonel Black.

His stern tone wiped the smiles off both their faces in an instant.

Amir quickly resumed his report. "In terms of threat level, Ms. Ryder appears to have more admirers than enemies. It's really Mr. Sterling's immense wealth—estimated at one and a half billion dollars—that makes him and his family a vulnerable target. Emily's kidnapping has already proved that the daughters are a tempting prize for any criminal organization. And, although the Corsican Mafia shouldn't be on the radar in the Indian Ocean, a secondary kidnapping attempt by extreme terrorists like the Seven Sabers of Somalia or an international crime syndicate, such as the Russian Bratva or the Chinese Triads, is a definite risk to consider."

"Any other potential threats?" asked Connor, very much aware that the colonel's frosty glare was still on him and Marc.

Amir nodded. "Just as in any tourist resort, robbery and theft are common in the Seychelles and the Maldives, especially around the harbors. Such crime tends to be opportunistic, so you'll have to stay alert. There's also the chance of harassment: the Sterling sisters are well recognized by the paparazzi, even more so since the kidnapping. But, surprisingly, Mr. Sterling's request for privacy has been honored. So far."

Amir paused in his threat report and finally looked up.

"Of course, there is one obvious danger when sailing the Indian Ocean." He brought up a photo of a skull and crossbones. "Pirates."

7

"You mean, like Captain Jack Sparrow?" said Jason, trying hard to suppress a grin.

"No, he means *real* pirates," replied Colonel Black. "Somali pirates, to be exact. And they're no joke. Forget your image of Johnny Depp with an eye patch and a parrot on his shoulder. Today's modern pirates use high-powered motorboats and are armed to the teeth with AK-47s and RPGs—rocket-propelled grenade launchers."

To prove the colonel's point, Amir played a jerky video clip of a narrow white-and-blue skiff cutting through the waves at high speed. Crouched on board were seven young African men wielding automatic rifles. The *crack* of gunfire could be heard above the furious roar of the skiff's outboard motor. A pirate in the bow held a rocket launcher trained on an unseen target. Connor and the others watched in stunned silence as the RPG scorched through the sky toward the cameraman. The picture juddered as the cameraman ducked in panic, but somehow he still managed to track the RPG's trajectory as it rocketed past the bridge of the ship.

The clip abruptly ended.

No one said a word, their image of the roguish yet lovable pirate from Hollywood movies shattered by this violent reality.

"Fortunately, a warship was within range and came to the cargo ship's rescue," the colonel revealed to everyone's relief. "But all too often these pirates do succeed in hijacking a vessel and holding it—and its crew—for ransom."

A graphics chart appeared on the screen with columns of colored blocks rapidly increasing in height like an ever-steepening staircase before plummeting in the last period.

"As you can see," said Amir, pointing to the screen, "the annual number of pirate attacks has soared in the last six years, from fifty-five to almost three hundred at its peak. Ransom demands have also risen. Five years ago the asking price was three hundred thousand dollars. Now it's as much as twenty *million* dollars and beyond."

Richie whistled through his teeth. "We're obviously in the wrong line of business."

"The problem is," said Amir, "success breeds success. Pirate gangs have become more organized and turned piracy into a full-blown business. Already this year there have been forty-two attempted hijackings and six ships taken hostage. A decrease from last year, but still worrying."

"If that's the case," questioned Ling, "why are we sailing in this area *at all*?"

"A fair point," agreed the colonel. "But, although the dangers are apparent, the risks are relatively low, as Amir will now explain."

Amir brought up Charley's map of the Indian Ocean again. "Attacks have occurred up to a thousand nautical miles from the Somalian coast, but the majority are concentrated along the International Recommended Transit Corridor in the Gulf of Aden." He pointed to a wide passage of water separating Somalia in the south from Yemen to the north. Then, indicating a stretch of ocean far to the southeast, he continued, "The planned route for Mr. Sterling's yacht won't go anywhere near the danger zone."

"But wasn't an elderly British couple taken hostage near the Seychelles some years back?" asked Connor, vaguely recalling the media coverage of their ordeal.

"You mean the Chandlers," answered Colonel Black. "They were *very* unlucky . . . Wrong place, wrong time. Since then there have been huge improvements in security. For example, NATO's counterpiracy mission, Operation Ocean Shield, and the setting up of a Regional Anti-Piracy Coordination Center in the Seychelles itself. These measures have curbed pirate activities significantly. Furthermore, it's relatively rare for the pirates to target a private yacht. The Somalis see the big money in the commercial vessels, because they have ransom insurance."

Amir nodded in agreement with the colonel. "It's true. Out of twenty thousand ships that pass through the transit corridor each year, only three hundred are ever attacked— and less than a quarter of those are captured. Of this number, just a handful have ever been private yachts. I worked out the actual odds." Amir scanned through his notes. "You have less than a one in ten thousand chance of being hijacked."

"Care to bet on it?" challenged Ling.

Amir gave a shrug. "Why not?"

8

"How can we trust you?"

Harry Gibb sat alone in the booth of the darkened restaurant. The disembodied voice was ominously threatening,
and he didn't dare look in the adjacent booth for fear of the
consequences.

"My enemy's enemy is my friend," he said with conviction.
"I want this as much as you."

"And you're willing to do whatever it takes?"

"Yes, yes. I want Sterling's life ruined. Just like he's de-
stroying mine!" Harry ground his teeth and clenched a fist in
fury at the thought of his collapsing career.

"Then we must hit him where it hurts: his family."

Harry felt a chill run through him. He stared at his fist and
slowly unclenched it. "R-really?" he questioned, his voice
quavering slightly. This was something he hadn't considered.
"You're not expecting *me* to do anything, are you? I'm not
that sort of person."

"Oh, Harry. It isn't as if you're an angel. I'm sure you've trampled over many innocent people on your way up the political ladder."

"Yes . . . but this is different."

The voice gave a hollow laugh. "No, Harry, this is no different. Politics is just as ruthless as revenge. It's just that with politics, you inflict harm *before* someone harms you. With revenge, at least it's after the act—a lot more honorable."

"I'm not sure I'm a hundred percent comfortable with this," Harry admitted, feeling the situation slipping out of his control. He only wanted to wreck Sterling's credibility and distract him from the campaign against him.

"Too late, Harry, you're in too deep now. And I can assure you, Mr. Sterling has no qualms about crushing you. But don't you worry—my men will do the dirty work. The question is, do you have the means to make it happen?"

"Y . . . yes," Harry replied, reaching into his jacket pocket and taking out a thick brown envelope, stuffed with five hundred crisp hundred-dollar bills.

A waiter eerily emerged from the shadows—or at least the man carried a waiter's tray. With a prominent tattoo and gorilla-like hands more suited to brutal work than simply serving food, the shadowy figure wasn't an obvious choice for a high-class establishment. Harry laid the envelope on the tray, and the "waiter" departed without a word.

"When will the 'campaign' begin?" he asked.

The adjacent booth was silent.

"I said, when will the plan commence?"

Still Harry got no answer. Warily, he rose from his seat and peeked over the divide. The booth was empty, except for a wireless loudspeaker on the table. His contact had never even been in the room with him.

Making his way past the coat check, Harry headed for the rear exit, where a bald bouncer wearing tinted sunglasses opened the fire door for him. Sunlight burst into the darkened corridor, dazzling Harry as if a police spotlight had caught him in the act. His heart racing, he scuttled out of the building and into the alleyway. The door clanged shut behind him with a booming finality that signaled there was no going back.

9

Connor's breath was labored as he sprinted headlong down the indoor track. His heart pounded in his chest, and his muscles burned. Jason was neck and neck with him. Elsa from Bravo team was close on their tail, as was Sean from Delta. The other recruits followed behind, some already struggling with the intense circuit.

"Come on, AMIR! Don't be the first to quit; a bodyguard needs to be fit!" bellowed Steve as he ran alongside them with apparent ease.

A towering slab of honed muscle, his limbs seemingly hewn from black marble, the ex–British Special Forces soldier was their unarmed-combat instructor and fitness coach. He'd summoned the three Guardian teams—Alpha, Bravo and Delta—to the gym for one of his infamous training sessions. To ensure their full commitment, he'd pitted them against one another, and with group pride at stake, no team wanted to be last.

"No pain, no gain!" called out Steve.

Connor reached the end of the shuttle sprint and dropped to the floor for fifty knuckle push-ups. Beside him, Jason pumped away like a jackhammer, clicking off reps every second. More students joined them, racing to catch up. Connor felt the burn in his triceps. But compared with the mental overload of an operational briefing, the physical exercise was a relief.

Amir dropped down next to him, the last of Alpha team. "I think . . . I might . . . die," he gasped in between push-ups.

"That's the spirit," said Steve, grinning a bright white smile at his student's torment. "It means you're putting in one hundred percent effort." He stood sentry over the teams, ensuring no one skipped a rep. "An unfit bodyguard is a liability. Not only to himself but also to other members of the team, and most of all to the Principal."

Jason was first to finish his push-ups and went straight into the next exercise—fifty stomach crunches.

"In an emergency, you'll need such strength to get you and your Principal out of the danger zone," continued their instructor as his students sweated and groaned on the floor. "Fatigue, on the other hand, will hamper your ability to make quick decisions and choose the right course of action."

"But we did a . . . ten-mile run . . . only yesterday!" panted Luciana, a dark-haired Brazilian girl from Delta team.

"Your fitness isn't about yesterday; it's about *today*," Steve lectured. "You must treat your fitness like a growing tree—water it every day; otherwise the tree will wilt. Just like you, Liam!"

He strode over to a boy on Bravo team who'd given up halfway through his push-ups.

"Would you trust your security to an unfit couch potato?"

Too out of breath to reply, Liam shook his head.

"Nor would I. Now let's see what you're made of. Keep going!"

His arms trembling with the effort, the boy resumed his exercise. Meanwhile, his teammate Elsa had completed her stomach crunches and was running to beat Jason to the chin-up bars. Connor was only a few paces behind. Charley, who'd used a vertical chest press and played catch with a medicine ball in place of push-ups and stomach crunches, powered her adapted sportschair over to a lowered chin-up bar. She fired off twenty reps before anyone else had even managed ten. Then, dropping back into her chair, she sped off along the track for another shuttle run—now the leader in the race.

As soon as she reached the end of the track, Steve announced, "Piggyback sprint."

This was met with groans of disbelief from the weary teams. But everyone dug in for what they prayed would be the final exercise. In Alpha team, Connor partnered with Amir, Jason ran with Richie, and Charley pulled herself up onto Ling's shoulders.

The teams raced down the hall. Ling managed to hold Alpha's lead; then Jason extended it. But Richie staggered under the weight of his brawny teammate.

"This is murder!" Richie moaned, gritting his teeth as Delta team swiftly passed him by.

"Winners train, losers complain," Steve growled. "When things go wrong and you need to run for cover while carrying your Principal, you'll be thankful for this exercise."

"I'll be thankful when it stops!" he gasped.

By the time it was Connor and Amir's turn, Alpha team had fallen into last place. Amir did his best to catch up, but had nothing left to give. It was a miracle he even managed to carry Connor over the line. Now they were almost ten seconds behind the leaders.

"It's all down to you," said Marc as a burned-out Amir clambered onto Connor's back.

Naturally fit from six years of martial arts training, Connor summoned up hidden reserves of energy and raced after the two rival teams. They quickly passed Bravo team as Elsa stumbled and went sprawling with her partner. But Delta still had the lead. And with only thirty meters left in the race, Connor had to dig deep.

"*Go! Go! Go!*" cried Amir, cheering him on as if he were a racehorse.

Connor could see that Luciana from Delta team, with Sean on her back, was fading fast. He pumped his legs and charged after them.

"*Come on!*" Amir urged.

They began to draw level. With victory almost in sight, Connor raced for the finish line.

Suddenly aware she was about to be passed, Luciana leaned forward like a jockey in the final few paces . . . and beat Alpha team by a nose.

Delta team cheered and high-fived Luciana in celebration of their slimmest of victories. Frustrated by their loss, Connor collapsed to his hands and knees in an exhausted heap, Amir rolling off him onto the floor.

"Good job, everyone," said Steve. "Take a break. I'll be back in ten minutes for combat practice."

As Steve passed Connor, he clapped a meaty hand on his shoulder. "You may have lost out this time, but that's what I call fighting fit."

Connor managed a weak smile. "Well, I'm fit for nothing now!"

10

Connor slumped on the bench and reached inside his training bag for his water bottle. Popping the cap, he almost drained it in one slug. Amir lay at his side, breathing hard, a weary arm draped across his forehead.

"I shouldn't have . . . made that joke . . . about hiring us too late," panted Amir.

Connor looked over at his friend, unable to believe Amir had the energy to dwell on the guardian assignment after such a grueling workout session. "The colonel's choice had nothing to do with your joke. He must've made up his mind before the briefing."

Amir propped himself up on one elbow, sweat dripping from his brow. "Then why didn't he choose me? I'm the only one in Alpha team who hasn't yet been on an assignment."

"Must be because you're so good with the tech stuff," said Marc, chucking Amir a towel. Amir wiped the sweat from his face, but his dejected expression remained.

Connor nodded encouragingly. "That's it! The colonel's playing to your strengths. During the mission, you'll be needed in HQ to maintain comms and run the IT. Remember last time, it was *you* and Bugsy who figured out the Cell-Finity bug."

"Great," said Amir without much enthusiasm. "So while you're off lounging in the Seychelles with Miss Swimsuit, I get stuck in wet Wales doing laps!"

"Look, Amir," said Connor, trying one last time to console his friend. "Ling was the most obvious choice."

"Why?"

"Because she's a girl."

"*Just* because I'm a girl!" remarked Ling, shooting daggers at Connor as she leaned against the ropes of the gym's boxing ring.

"No . . . I didn't mean it like that," Connor protested.

"Whatever, *Boss*," she replied, her tone laced with sarcasm.

Connor sighed. This didn't bode well for their forthcoming assignment. "Let me explain—"

"Be my guest," she said, lifting the ropes of the boxing ring and inviting him to join her.

"But we just did laps!" exclaimed Connor.

"Is that your excuse?" Ling gave him a withering look, somehow still appearing as fresh as a daisy herself. "Or is it because I'm a *girl*, so you don't want to fight?"

Connor shook his head, wondering how he was going to

avoid the sparring challenge. Although he was a black belt in jujitsu and kickboxing, that didn't mean he took a match with Ling lightly. At their very first encounter, she'd demonstrated that she was a supremely tough combatant. In Amir's words, "Ling *always* wins her fights."

It was as if she had something to prove. And Ling wasn't to be dissuaded now. She bounced nimbly on her feet and pulled on the sparring gloves Jason offered.

"I don't think Connor's up for it," Jason remarked, handing Ling her mouth guard while eyeballing Connor. "I hope he's not going to be a liability on your mission."

Members of Bravo and Delta teams were soon drawn to the ring by the excitement of a challenge fight.

"I thought you were the Battle of Britain Kickboxing Champion," remarked Luciana, still gloating over her victory. "Let's see you prove it."

"Go on, Connor," urged Sean. "You know how 'Lightning Ling' only sees sense in the ring!"

Connor looked to Amir for a way out. But his friend just shrugged. "You don't seem to have much choice," he said. "You'll have to play to *your* strengths."

Despite his exhausted state, Connor ducked under the rope, entered the ring, put on a pair of sparring gloves and turned to face his opponent—

An explosive jab almost took his head off. Only blind instinct enabled him to spin away in time. A right hook came flying in, and Connor had to weave sharply aside again. Ling certainly wasn't waiting around for an official start to the fight.

"So the colonel's choice," said Ling, launching a round-house kick to his thigh, "has nothing to do with my previous experience?"

"Of course it does!" Connor grunted, blocking the kick with his shin and countering with a front kick.

Ling skipped out of range, then came back in with a body hook punch to his ribs. "Or my surveillance skills—?"

Connor grimaced as the strike hit home. Ling might be small, but she was *lightning* fast.

"Or my fighting ability?" she demanded.

Like a whirling dervish, Ling came at him with a flurry of kicks and punches. Connor fought hard to defend him-self. He ducked her spinning backfist, blocked her cross and evaded her crescent kick. As he retreated from Ling's re-lentless onslaught, Luciana goaded him from the ringside, "Some champion you are, Connor!"

Needled by the taunt and wanting to get a word in edge-wise with Ling, Connor now went on the attack.

"Ling, I meant you got the job," he replied with a blistering combination of jab, cross and uppercut, "because . . . our two Principals . . . are girls. It therefore makes sense"—he almost floored Ling with a backfist—"to have a *female* guardian."

Ling was driven into the corner by a pounding side kick

to the chest. She tried to fight her way out, but Connor kept her trapped with a series of punishing body blows.

"You can go places I can't," he said. Ling, taking the hits, fought hard to escape, but Connor maintained the pressure. He still had more to say. "And their protection is supposed to be low profile, so a *girl* bodyguard will be even less noticeable than a boy."

Connor grunted as Ling thrust a front kick into his gut, forcing him backward.

"Is that low profile enough for you?" Ling asked, grinning and relishing the buzz of the fight.

Connor ignored her and retaliated with a front kick of his own that propelled Ling back into the ring's corner pad.

"So, apart from your core skills, being a *girl* makes you the obvious choice," explained Connor, moving to finish her off with a couple of head shots.

But Ling displayed some nifty footwork and escaped the corner. "Fair enough," she said, with a disarming smile. "My mistake. Please accept my apology."

She backed off from the fight, and Connor dropped his guard. *Finally* he'd got through to Ling. "Of course I do. We're teammates. I didn't mean any offense—"

Ling spun on her heel, shot out a leg and caught him smack on the jaw with a spinning hook kick. "There's my apology."

Connor went down like a sack of potatoes, his last conscious thought *Ling* always *wins her fights.*

11

Harry Gibb hurried through the deserted government office. He knew even his most eager fellow civil servants wouldn't show their faces until at least 8:00 a.m. That gave him two hours of solitude. Still, he glanced nervously around before unlocking the main archive room and ducking inside.

Flicking on the switch, he waited for the fluorescent strip lights to cast their stark white glare over the rows and rows of gray filing cabinets. Each one was a carbon copy of the next, impossible to tell apart, but Harry knew exactly what he was looking for. Heading straight over to the sixth cabinet in the third row, he pulled out a thick binder of documents marked MINING RIGHTS, GOLDFIELDS, WA.

Despite everything being stored digitally nowadays, there was *always* a paper trail in government. He'd been careful to remove any evidence from his computer, but these damning documents were the remaining crumbs that could lead to him and his under-the-table dealings.

Yet he *wouldn't* destroy the files. The contents of this folder, detailing his co-conspirators, were his insurance policy. Harry Gibb knew that those who had profited from the shady deals also had a vested interest in protecting his reputation. If he went down, so would they.

Smiling to himself, Harry closed the filing cabinet, switched off the light and locked the archive room. Clutching the files to his chest, he scurried across to his office and bolted inside. Only when he'd secured the door behind him did he feel safe in his domain.

Turning to his desk, Harry almost jumped out of his skin when he discovered a man in a gray suit sitting in his chair.

"M-my secretary didn't mention any meetings this morning," he blustered.

"She doesn't know of *this* meeting," replied the man. "No one does."

The uninvited guest did not get up or introduce himself. He just studied Harry with unblinking eyes that seemed chiseled from ice.

"Who are you?" Harry demanded, gathering his wits and becoming angry. "Are you a reporter? Get out of my chair!"

The man was indifferent to Harry's outrage. "I represent a certain investor."

"And who might that be?" Harry challenged.

"Your primary investor."

"I don't know what you're talking about," said Harry. He felt himself becoming flustered. There was something deeply unsettling about this man. He was like a spider crawling across his skin, and Harry wanted him gone. "If you don't leave right now, I'll call security."

"I'd advise against that."

"Are you threatening me?"

The man sat as still as a block of stone, his silence more unnerving than any reply. Then he said, "Equilibrium."

"What?" snapped Harry, frowning in disbelief.

"You heard me."

"Ahh," said Harry, relaxing slightly. This man *had* to be from his key investor. There could be no other way he'd have known of the organization's name. It had taken Harry weeks to discover it for himself—Equilibrium, the parent investor behind all those false "shell" companies who'd invested in the mining rights.

Feeling once more in charge of the situation, Harry strode over and dropped the thick binder onto his desk.

"I'm dealing with the problem," he said, waving a dismissive hand in the man's direction. "Equilibrium need not be concerned. Neither their existence nor their involvement will be revealed. Plans are in place to handle Mr. Sterling and his prying newspaper."

"But *you're* familiar with Equilibrium."

"Of course," said Harry. "I was *thorough* in selecting my investors."

"And are they fully protected from the current crisis?"

"Oh yes," Harry assured him. "I've erased all evidence from my computer records."

"So have I," said the man, pulling a tiny USB drive from the back of Harry's computer. "A malware virus has just wiped your hard drive."

"You can't do that!" exclaimed Harry.

"And what about those files there?" asked the man, ignoring Harry's protest and nodding at the thick wad of documents on his desk.

"These? They're just an insurance policy."

"Hmm, that's the problem," said the man, adjusting the crisp white cuffs of his shirt. "Not only do you know Equilibrium's name but you possess evidence of its existence."

"I . . . I'm not going to expose Equilibrium's involvement in this. The file is just for my own protection from the other parties. They know nothing about Equilibrium," said Harry, suddenly feeling a chill run down his spine from the man's sinister casualness. "Trust me. I'm a man of my word."

"You're a politician," the other corrected sharply, his ice-pick eyes fixing him with a contemptuous look. "But I'll take your word . . . for what it's worth."

Without further discussion, the man stood and left. Once

the door closed on him, the room seemed to breathe again.

Although the man was gone, Harry felt a familiar tightening in his chest. He unlocked his desk drawer and pulled out his heart pills. With an unsteady hand, he unscrewed the bottle cap and shook out two pills. As he swallowed them, he felt a burning sensation that continued down his throat, into his stomach . . . and kept spreading.

His heart stabbed with pain, his throat constricted, his breath became short and pained, and the tablets fell out of his hands, spilling all over the floor.

Thinking he needed more medication, Harry fell to his knees and hunted for his pills. He fumbled around, scattering beta-blockers across the floor as his heart was seized in a viselike grip. Harry rolled on the floor, his lips foaming with spittle. He clawed at the little white tablets strewn around him. But his body was racked with pain, fire raging through his veins.

"H . . . h . . . *help!*" he moaned. "*Heeelp . . .*"

The man in the gray suit reentered the room.

"*P . . . p . . . please,*" Harry begged, reaching out.

But the man merely observed Harry writhe on the carpet with an almost inhuman detachment. Harry's eyes bulged, unable to comprehend the man's indifference. A sharp pain speared his chest. He shuddered once more, then lay still.

The man in the gray suit checked Harry Gibb's body for

signs of life. Satisfied, he picked up the documents from the desk, the medicine bottle and the poisoned heart pills from the floor. Quietly closing the office door behind him, he headed for the emergency exit, the first phase of his mission accomplished.

12

"Enter," barked Colonel Black.

Taking a deep breath, Connor stepped inside the colonel's office. An old-fashioned wood-paneled affair with high-back red leather chairs and a heavy mahogany desk the size of a small boat, it reminded Connor of M's office in the old Bond movies. Yet, despite the room's antique appearance, it was equipped with the most advanced state-of-the-art technology. Built within the desk was a discreet multicore computer, its slim glass monitor retractable into a hidden recess. A super-thin LED display hung on the wall, broadcasting international news feeds and up-to-the-minute security intel. There was a high-definition videoconferencing system enabling the colonel to govern Guardian operations worldwide, and hidden surveillance cameras provided total security for the room.

As Connor approached the desk, the colonel lowered his monitor and raised an inquiring eyebrow.

"That's an impressive black eye," he remarked.

Connor managed a pained smile. "An *apology* from Ling during combat training."

The colonel grunted in amusement. "Glad to see you're getting along so well. Let's hope the bruise has faded by the time of your assignment. It wouldn't be professional to turn up looking like some street brawler."

Connor nodded. "I'm putting ice on it. But it wasn't exactly my fault. I don't think Ling likes me."

The colonel looked surprised. "Whatever makes you say that?"

"She's . . ." Connor wasn't sure how to phrase it and didn't want to sound like he was whining. "She's *waspish* with me. Has been since my return from America."

"Ling can be like that," replied the colonel, brushing away Connor's concerns with a wave of his hand. "I'm aware that her social skills require a touch more finesse. But she comes from a tough background."

Connor frowned. "What do you mean?"

Colonel Black sucked his teeth and shook his head. "Not my place to say. But don't concern yourself over whether Ling likes you or not. I'm confident she respects you. And that's what counts on a mission."

"How can you be so sure?" asked Connor.

The colonel offered a wry grin. "She wouldn't want to fight you if she didn't respect you."

He indicated for Connor to take a seat. "Now, why did you want to see me? I'm sure it's not just to show me your black eye."

Perching on one of the red leather chairs, Connor summoned up his courage. Unable to meet Colonel Black's piercing gaze, he admitted, "I . . . don't think I'm ready for this assignment."

"Nonsense," snorted the colonel. "I've just been reviewing your progress. That video of you and the Dumpster was inspirational. I'm even considering showing it to the other teams."

"But I *failed* to protect my Principal."

"No," he instantly corrected Connor, "you learned what you should do next time to *prevent* that from happening. Failure is the key to success; each mistake teaches us something. So when you're out in the field all that training comes together and you avoid such mistakes."

"But I feel like I'm rushing too fast into my next assignment," Connor argued. "I've only just gotten over my injury"—he rubbed his thigh where the assassin's bullet had struck—"and I've hardly had any advanced training."

"Don't worry. You'll get more training once you're out

there," assured Colonel Black. "The ship security officer on board Mr. Sterling's yacht is a former member of the Australian SAS. I've checked his background. Brad Harding is a good man. He'll back you up, and he's agreed to teach you and Ling the necessary maritime security skills."

"But . . ." Connor stopped. He realized he was losing this line of argument, so he went straight to the heart of the matter. "But I'm worried my first assignment was just a fluke. Beginner's luck."

The colonel fixed Connor with an incredulous stare. "If that's the case, you have the luck of the gods, since you protected your Principal on *three* separate occasions. Listen, Operation Hidden Shield was a challenging assignment for any bodyguard. *Don't doubt your abilities.* You've proved that your reactions are second to none. Without question, you're a chip off your father's block."

"But I'm *not* my father," said Connor firmly. "I bet he never doubted himself like this."

Colonel Black leaned back in his chair, pressed his fingers together and gazed thoughtfully at Connor. "I'll tell you a story about your father."

Connor's ears suddenly perked up. This was one of the reasons he'd joined Guardian in the first place. To learn more about his dad and the secret life he'd led as an SAS operative. Colonel Black, having been in his father's squadron, was the key to much of his hidden past.

"We were based in Afghanistan at the time, when two SAS troopers were seized by the Taliban who had infiltrated the Afghan police," the colonel began. "Our commander immediately initiated a rescue operation. We knew that the hostages were still being held in the police station but that they could be spirited away at any moment. Our unit was all ready to go in when we got word from Operation Command that permission for the rescue *hadn't* been granted by the Ministry of Defense. There were apparently more important matters at stake than the lives of two soldiers . . . *diplomatic* reasons."

Colonel Black's face grew thunderous at the memory of such political betrayal.

"The men were furious, none more so than your father, Justin. He lived by the decree that 'no man is left behind on the battlefield.' So, as the unit's captain, he decided to launch the rescue mission anyway."

"He disobeyed a direct order?" said Connor, shocked.

The colonel nodded. "I know Justin harbored doubts about whether he should go ahead with it. After all, his actions were tantamount to mutiny. Failure would result in catastrophic consequences, not just militarily but diplomatically. But his priority was the captured soldiers."

Connor nodded and smiled. "That sounds like my father. My mother often said he always put others first."

"That he did. Your father and the rest of his unit blasted

their way into the police station. The soldiers fanned out, firing stun grenades and clearing each of the rooms in turn. As your father entered the last cell, he was confronted by a Taliban militant slicing a knife across one of the hostage's throats."

Connor swallowed, instinctively putting a hand to his own throat at the gruesome image.

"Your father's reactions were second to none. He dispatched the militant with a single shot to the head."

"What about the hostage?" asked Connor, breathless.

Colonel Black reached up and pulled his shirt collar down to reveal the long white scar that circled his neck.

"He survived," the colonel said with a smile. "That's why I have such faith in you, Connor, to protect others—just like your father protected *me*."

13

Connor pulled on his board shorts and stuffed his belongings into the locker. Stifling a yawn, he made his way through the empty changing room to the pool. Never in his life had he gotten up so early to go swimming. In fact, he'd rather do an early morning run than a swim any day—and on a Sunday, sleeping late was preferable to both. But, with his forthcoming operation being at sea, Connor figured he needed to work on his swimming skills.

As he stepped from the changing rooms, he caught sight of an abandoned wheelchair lying upended by the side of the pool. He glanced around, but nobody was to be seen.

"Charley?" he called, his voice bouncing off the white tiled walls and echoing his concern.

No one answered. Then he spotted her body at the bottom of the pool.

Connor tossed aside his towel and dived in, the chilly

water shocking his system. Opening his eyes, the underwater scene was a blur of blue shadows and refracted sunlight from the pool's glass ceiling. He spied her black swimsuit against the white tiles and swam hard toward her. Grabbing hold of an outstretched arm, he kicked upward with all his strength.

Charley's head bobbed to the surface at the same time as his.

"Hey!" she spluttered. "What're you doing?"

Connor blinked the water away from his eyes and stared at her. "You're okay?"

"Of course I am," she replied, floating easily at his side. "I was practicing holding my breath. Useful if you're pinned down by a wave while surfing."

"B-but I thought . . . you were drowning."

Charley crinkled her nose in puzzlement. "Why on earth would you think that?"

"Because . . ." Connor glanced toward her wheelchair.

Charley immediately gave him *that* look. The one that said, *Don't judge me by my chair.*

"Sorry," Connor mumbled, treading water. "My mistake . . . I haven't had breakfast yet, not thinking straight," he added by way of a lame excuse.

"Forget it," she replied with half a smile. "It's kind of sweet that you dived to my rescue, though. A true bodyguard reaction. The chair tipped over as I got into the water. I must have forgotten to apply the brake. But I can handle myself in the water."

"Of course you can," he said, annoyed at himself for forgetting that she'd once been a surfing champion. "Still, isn't it a bit dangerous to be swimming on your own?"

"I could say the same about you," she countered, a steely flash in her eyes. "Since I've been in a wheelchair, I've had countless people tell me what I can and can't do. They see my disability as inability. But I soon realized the only person who can place restrictions on me is *me*."

"You're right," Connor replied, holding up a hand in apology. "I was just . . . worried about you."

Her expression softened slightly. "What are you doing here anyway? You're never in the pool—not at this time, anyway."

"I'm trying to prepare myself for Operation Gemini. And you?"

"Swimming, of course!" she said, laughing, her mood lightening as she lay back in the water. She splashed, twirling effortlessly with a single stroke of her arm. "This is the one place where I can forget about my disability. All day long I'm like a prisoner in that chair. So this pool offers me the most freedom I can experience since losing the use of my legs."

Connor didn't know what to say to this. He still had no idea what had happened to Charley on that fateful assignment the previous year. But he didn't press her for details. No doubt Charley would tell him in her own time, if she ever wanted to.

"I virtually grew up in the ocean," she continued. "For me, swimming is second nature. Now it's the one thing I can do free of my chair. Yet"—Charley spun to look directly at Connor, and he saw the fierce burn of determination in her gaze—"my real dream is to surf again."

She grinned at the impossibility of the challenge she'd set herself. "And when that day comes, I intend to be ready for it."

Ducking her head beneath the water, she swam off down the length of the pool. Connor watched her speed away with the grace of a dolphin and could only admire her resolve. He realized Charley was the sort of person who, when faced with a barrier, wouldn't stop and turn around; she'd just smash through it. Inspired by her spirit, Connor questioned how he could doubt his own abilities, when Charley with her disability wouldn't even let doubt enter her mind.

With a new resolve, Connor put his head down and swam after her.

But after only eight lengths, he found himself completely out of breath and his pulse racing. Gasping for air, he splashed the last few yards and clung to the lip of the pool to recover.

"It's your breathing technique that's the problem," said Charley as she toweled herself off poolside.

Connor glanced over. Blessed with slender limbs, tanned golden skin and beach-blond hair, Charley looked the quintessential Californian beach girl. With her legs dangling in the pool, it was hard to imagine that she had a disability at all.

"Your stroke is basically fine," she continued, "but you're trying to inhale *and* exhale when your head's above the water. Exhale *under* the water. Then when you go to breathe, you only have to inhale."

"Okay," said Connor, nodding his appreciation.

Charley put down her towel and pulled herself into her chair. "Next time I'll teach you how to breathe *bilaterally*. That'll make a massive difference in your swimming technique. You'll be able to cut through the water like an arrow."

Wondering whether he'd heard right, Connor tried to clear his ears. "Next time?"

"Yes," said Charley, beaming. She flipped the towel over her shoulder and wheeled away. "I can't leave a job half finished. Meet me in the pool tomorrow."

"What time?" called Connor as she disappeared into the girls' changing room.

"Same time," her voice echoed back.

Grateful as he was for her training offer, Connor groaned at the thought of another early morning start. *Why couldn't my assignment have been on dry land?*

14

Dust swirled in the hot dry air as a white-and-chrome Land Cruiser bumped its way down Hobyo's unpaved street. In the furnace of midafternoon, the Somalian harbor town was largely deserted, except for a few scrawny children kicking a soccer ball made of plastic bags.

Sharif, a potbellied Somali with a thin mustache, gazed through his vehicle's blacked-out windows at the crumbling concrete buildings beyond. Some were whitewashed, and others matched the dull brown of the road. All were topped with green corrugated tin roofs that had warped under the glare of the African sun.

The driver honked his horn, and a goat, bleating indignantly, trotted out of the path of the oncoming 4×4. Turning a corner, the Land Cruiser entered the central square, where, unexpectedly, the town was bustling with life. A throng of people crowded outside a two-story building with flaking yellow walls, pockmarked by bullet holes.

The Land Cruiser ground to a halt beside three other 4×4s that were haphazardly parked in the middle of the road, their stereos blaring reggae-inspired tunes. Several young men in T-shirts and *ma'awis* wrapped around their waists were slumped beneath a tree. Chewing green khat leaves, their AK-47 machine guns cradled in their laps, they eyed the Land Cruiser with mild suspicion but made no move to investigate.

Sharif clambered out of the air-conditioned cocoon of the vehicle, his blue cotton shirt instantly sticking to him in the sapping heat as he strode over to the gathered mob.

"*Ii warran?*" he asked a woman wearing a black headscarf.

The young woman, her face dark and smooth as ebony, grinned at him. "A ransom payout!" she replied in Somali, and held up a slip of paper. "I'm waiting to collect my share. I invested my ex-husband's rocket-propelled grenade in the company."

Other fortunate investors, who'd gambled their money, weapons or belongings with the successful pirate gang, pushed and jostled their way forward to make their claims. But not everyone was jubilant. An elderly woman in a long blue *jilbaab* squatted in the dirt, her eyes red raw with tears.

"Has . . . anyone news . . . of my son?" she sobbed, raising her hands to the heavens.

Another woman crouched at her side, trying to offer comfort. "I'm sure he's still at sea—"

Ignoring the old woman's sorrow, Sharif shouldered his way through the crowd into the former mayor's office that now housed the pirates' "stock exchange," a facility for raising funds for hijack operations. Six brokers were dealing with the numerous claims of the town's investors as well as welcoming new investments.

Sharif approached a round-faced man wearing gold-rimmed glasses. Sitting at a rickety wooden desk, the broker welcomed him with a gap-toothed grin.

"*Soo dhowow!*" he said in greeting. "Cousin, please sit down." He gestured to a battered plastic chair. "How can I help you?"

Sharif immediately got down to business. "I represent a client who wishes to invest in a pirate gang."

"You mean a *'maritime company*,'" corrected the broker with a knowing wink.

"Ah . . . yes, of course," Sharif agreed amiably, although both men knew what they were really talking about. "And he only wants the best, the most reliable."

The broker didn't even pause before replying. "That'll be Oracle and his men."

Flipping to a fresh page in his battered ledger, the broker licked the tip of his pencil, wrote the date and scored a line down one side. He glanced up at Sharif. "What does your client have to invest? Weapons? Supplies? Cash?"

"Cash. And moreover he wants to be the *sole* investor in an operation."

The broker's eyes widened, gleaming like silver coins in his black moon-face. "I trust your client has deep pockets ... Start-up costs are a minimum of thirty thousand dollars."

Sharif nodded and placed a blue sports bag on the table. "There's fifty thousand. My client wishes to ensure the 'maritime company' has the best resources for the job."

The broker unzipped the bag and licked his lips at the sight of five large bundles of crisp hundred-dollar bills.

"I'll contact Oracle right away," he said, rezipping the bag. But as he went to take it, Sharif grabbed his wrist and locked eyes with the broker.

"My client expects results."

The broker gave Sharif a regretful smile. "Of course I respect such a request, but in this business, as you well know, we can offer no guarantees. Hijacking a ship is risky business."

"Then this should reduce the risk," said Sharif, handing the broker a large brown envelope.

The broker started to open it.

"No," said Sharif. "For Oracle's eyes only."

The broker held up his hand in apology. "I only wished to note its contents. The return on a successful hijack-and-ransom is usually ten times the amount invested." Placing the unopened envelope in the bag, he then carefully wrote down the items in his ledger. "Whom shall I name as the official investor? Yourself, Sharif?"

"No, I'm merely the middleman. No name. Just date it," instructed Sharif.

The broker raised an eyebrow at this, but nonetheless did as instructed. He glanced up as he wrote. "Is your client trustworthy?"

Sharif shrugged. "He's rich. And pays cash in advance."

"Then who needs trust?" the broker said, laughing. He tore a strip of paper from the bottom of his ledger. "Your receipt."

Sharif took the scrap of paper. "Thank you, cousin. *Nabadeey*," he said, bidding him farewell.

Leaving the bustling "stock exchange," Sharif crossed the dusty square and clambered back into the Land Cruiser.

"It's done," he said in English, handing his client the receipt.

The man in the back pocketed the paper slip without a word.

15

"Mayday, Mayday, Mayday! This is motor yacht Athena, Athena, Athena. *Mayday* Athena. *My position is South three degrees, fifty-two minutes, twenty-three seconds, East fifty-five degrees, thirty-four minutes, forty-two seconds, approximately five miles southwest of Denis Island. We have hit submerged object and are sinking. I have four people on board. We require immediate assistance. Abandoning to life raft. Over."*

The VHF radio crackled loudly with static.

No one responded to the distress call. Nor was a response expected.

Ling, who'd sent the message, sat safe and sound in Alpha team's classroom at Guardian headquarters, miles from any sinking ship. She turned to Bugsy, radio mic in hand. "Why does everything have to be repeated three times?"

Their surveillance and communications tutor, a bald man with the stocky build of a wrestler, held up two stubby fingers. "First, to ensure that the message is heard accurately. And second, to distinguish it from other radio chatter."

He lowered the radio's volume and faced the rest of the team.

"Knowing how to make a Mayday call is a vital skill for any crew member aboard a boat. It can mean the difference between life and death at sea." His sharp, beady eyes flicked across to Connor. "Summarize the Mayday procedure for me."

Connor glanced at his notes.

"Turn on VHF radio, check power, press and hold the red Distress button for five seconds—"

"Good. Now, Amir, what does this action do?" interjected Bugsy.

Amir was quick to respond. "It broadcasts a digital alert to all DSC-equipped craft as well as the local coast guard. This will include your MMSI—the unique number identifying your craft—along with your position and the time."

Bugsy gave his student a big thumbs-up, and Amir beamed. "Jason," Bugsy continued, "what if there's no response within fifteen seconds?"

"Uh . . . repeat the distress call."

"That's right. But this time by voice, just as Ling did." Bugsy turned to Richie, who was gazing out the window with a blank expression. "Richie, what VHF channel should you transmit on?"

Richie fumbled for an answer. "Um . . . Ten?"

"No, Channel Sixteen!" snapped Bugsy, tapping the dial on the radio that clearly indicated this. "Pay attention. Just because you're not going on this mission, Richie, doesn't mean you won't need this knowledge in the future. All distress, urgency and safety signals are transmitted by international agreement on VHF Channel Sixteen. Make a note of it."

With a grudging effort, Richie opened his laptop and typed the information down.

Bugsy tutted at his student, then resumed his questioning. "So, Marc, what must you check before sending a verbal Mayday?"

Marc rubbed his temple, trying to jog his memory. Then he clicked his fingers as he remembered. "That the radio is switched to *high power* to transmit."

Bugsy nodded. "Connor, what is the official format of the Mayday call?"

Connor didn't need to check his notes this time. "Repeat 'Mayday' and the name of the vessel three times, then give your position, nature of the emergency, the number of people on board and what assistance you need, and finish by saying 'over.'"

Bugsy fired more questions around the room, allowing *no one* the opportunity to tune out his lesson again. Once satisfied that Alpha team knew the protocol inside out, he announced, "One important proviso about VHF radios—they have a limited line-of-sight range. In real terms, that's about forty miles from a coastal station, but only ten miles between two yachts. So, considering the size of the oceans, this is by no means a foolproof distress system."

"How about using a smartphone instead?" Amir suggested.

Ling laughed. "You're at sea, stupid! Where will you get a signal?"

"Actually, cell phones can be used for requesting help," said Bugsy. "In areas of little or seemingly no signal, a text might still stand a good chance of getting through."

Amir gave Ling a triumphant look and waved his cell phone in her face. "See! It would work."

"Teacher's pet," she muttered, her eyes narrowing.

"Loser," shot back Amir.

Ling made a grab for his smartphone. "Watch it or I'll stick that phone where there's *definitely* no signal!"

"Settle down, you two," said Bugsy, wagging a finger at their childish squabbling. "Ling's got a point, though. The signal range is limited to the coastal areas. Also, only one person hears your call, and a cell phone can't be homed in on as easily as a VHF transmission."

Ling stuck her tongue out at Amir in smug victory.

Bugsy frowned at her but continued with his lecture. "That's why most boats are equipped with satellite systems featuring voice, data, fax and GMDSS capabilities."

"What's GMDSS?" asked Jason, struggling to make notes fast enough.

"Global Maritime Distress and Safety System. It's a highly sophisticated worldwide distress system that delivers emergency, safety and other communications, such as weather warnings and search-and-rescue messages—"

The class bell rang for lunch, and like all schoolkids, Alpha team began to pack up with impatient urgency.

"Just one more thing," said Bugsy, holding up a bright yellow plastic cylinder with a light and a short aerial at one end. "This is an emergency position–indicating radio beacon. It transmits a distress signal to satellites and relays the information to a rescue coordination center. EPIRBs are pretty cool gadgets, since they automatically activate upon immersion in water and have a float-free bracket if the vessel sinks."

Bugsy placed the EPIRB on the desk for the class to examine. Then he stowed away his laptop, popped a piece of chewing gum into his mouth and headed out the door.

Alpha team gathered their belongings and filed past the EPIRB, giving it the once-over.

Jason picked it up and regarded Connor. "Let's pray there aren't any Maydays on your mission."

"I'm with you there," said Connor. Then he caught the odd expression on Jason's face. "Hey, what do you mean by that?"

"Well, you got shot last time, didn't you?"

Nettled by the implied criticism, Connor held his rival's gaze. "And I heard that on your Caribbean assignment you got second-degree sunburn!"

A moment of tension hung between them. Then Jason's mouth broke into a wide grin.

"Fair point," he chuckled, putting down the EPIRB and clapping a meaty arm around Connor's shoulders. "That was rather stupid of me, wasn't it?" He glanced in Ling's direction as she left the classroom with Amir, the two of them now laughing together. "Look, just watch Ling's back for me. That's all I'm asking."

"I think she can look after herself," replied Connor, indicating the faded shadow of his black eye from the previous week.

"Sure, she can," agreed Jason, "but if something goes wrong . . . you've only got each other to depend on." His earth-brown eyes searched Connor's face as if looking for a weakness. Then, with a final encouraging squeeze of his arm, he let go and shouldered his bag. "I hear you and Ling are flying out to Australia to meet the girls before the trip?"

Connor nodded. "Yes, by request of Mr. Sterling."

"Well, enjoy my home turf," he said with genuine warmth, heading for lunch. He paused a moment in the doorway as if remembering something. "But watch out for dropbears."

"Dropbears?" queried Connor.

"Yeah, vicious little creatures. Like koalas, only with teeth. My uncle was savaged by one last summer," Jason explained. "They hang in treetops and attack their prey by dropping onto their heads from above. Just be careful is all I'm saying."

"Thanks for the heads-up," said Connor.

"No worries," replied Jason, smiling.

16

Connor and Ling entered the logistics supply room to find Amir already there. He stood behind the desk with an eager look on his face as if his birthday had come early.

"I've been waiting all morning to hand over your go-bags," he said.

Unable to contain his excitement any longer, Amir produced two black-and-fluorescent-yellow backpacks and laid them ceremonially on the table. "I've customized them specifically for Operation Gemini."

"Well, no one's going to lose these in a hurry!" remarked Ling, eyeing the lurid yellow dubiously.

"That's the point," said Amir. "Ultra-reflective strips on the front and shoulder straps for maximum visibility at sea. A high-powered LED beacon for emergencies." Amir indicated a tiny plastic dome beside the top grab handle. "And these bags even have a mini-SART sewn into the lining!"

Amir looked up expectantly, waiting for them to share

in his enthusiasm. Connor and Ling exchanged bemused glances. Amir rolled his eyes.

"Don't you two know anything? SART? Search-and-rescue transponder." He pointed to a bulging seam with an activation tag. "The slim tube inside contains a small, battery-powered receiver and transmitter that operates on the 9-GHz frequency."

"You've still lost us, I'm afraid," admitted Connor.

"That frequency, 9 GHz, is the frequency . . . of X-band radar . . . on a ship," Amir said slowly, as if explaining to two nursery school–aged kids. "If you get into difficulties at sea, the transponder sends out a locating signal. Usually these gizmos are on life rafts and about the size of a two-liter water bottle. Bugsy, however, has managed to miniaturize it. The downside is that the battery has only an eight-hour life span and its range is less than five nautical miles. Still, it could make all the difference in a search-and-rescue operation."

Amir unclipped the top section of the backpack and began to unroll the opening.

"No zips mean no leakage," he said, explaining the unusual roll-top design. "This means the go-bags are fully waterproof and fully submersible. As long as you aren't carrying rocks, they'll even float!"

Amir patted the go-bags proudly as if they were his favored pets.

"Do they have a foldout liquid body-armor panel like before?" Connor asked.

Amir's expression fell a little. "Unfortunately not," he admitted. "We couldn't fit an additional panel inside. But the back section itself *is* bulletproof."

"That's good," said Connor. He didn't wish to dampen Amir's spirits, but the foldout panel had been a key factor in saving his and his Principal's life during his first mission. A single panel, although still useful, would barely cover him, let alone his Principal.

Amir reached into the bags and produced a pair of phones enclosed in bright orange neoprene covers.

"Your smartphones, upgraded to the newest operating system and virus-protection software." He arched an eyebrow in Connor's direction. "No danger of Cell-Finity bugs this time."

"Glad to hear it," said Connor as he weighed the phone in his hand and examined the unusual cover. "A bit bulky, isn't it?"

"It was a trade-off," said Amir, shrugging apologetically. "We've waterproofed the phone with a spray-on microlayer, but to produce a buoyant cover we had to compromise on size."

"I suppose it's better than losing it at the bottom of the sea," said Ling cheerily.

Connor pressed his thumb to the screen, triggering the fingerprint security system. He examined the display of apps: Advanced Mapping, Tracker, Face Recognition, Mission Status, Threat Level, SOS . . . "I'm glad to see your SOS app is still on here."

"Of course," Amir said, beaming. "Version two. Improved battery life. Also, it allows for short message transfer as well as location data."

Amir dug out the rest of the go-bag's contents.

"You'll have all your usual gear: first-aid kits, earpieces with a built-in mic for covert communication with each other, prepaid credit cards—"

"Now, that's more like it." Ling grinned, snatching up a card. "Shopping time!"

"You'll need expert surveillance skills to find a shop in the middle of the Indian Ocean," Amir said, laughing.

"You forget airport duty-free," Ling replied with a devious wink, nudging Connor with her elbow.

Amir handed them each a pile of clothes. "Here's your Guardian-issued gear: baseball hat, shorts, T-shirts, polo shirt . . . all fire-retardant, stab-proof and, of course, bullet-proof," he said, looking up at Connor.

"Don't worry, I'll definitely be wearing these," said Connor, holding up and inspecting the pocketed blue polo shirt. It still amazed him that such soft, thin fabric could stop a bullet from a handgun or the sharpened steel point of a knife.

"Is there a bulletproof bikini for me?" asked Ling.

Amir searched through her pile of clothes. "Uh, no, sorry."

A smirk appeared on Ling's lips. "I was only joking."

Amir reddened as it dawned on him how ridiculous such an item would be. "Oh, very funny." He pulled a slim black flashlight from the go-bag. "By the way, Bugsy's supplied you with a new flashlight."

Amir pressed the button, and a glaringly bright green laser strobe flashed out.

"Hey, watch it!" exclaimed Ling, shielding her eyes. "You almost blinded me."

"That's kinda the point of it," said Amir, grinning like a Cheshire cat at his retaliation. "It's a Dazzler."

"A what?"

"A nonlethal weapon that temporarily blinds or disorients your enemy."

"Seems pretty lethal to me," said Ling as she blinked away tears.

"Well, it won't kill anyone, and it works as a standard flashlight too," Amir explained, putting the Dazzler back in the bag. "Anyway, at the other end of the spectrum, so to speak, are your sunglasses."

"It's all right—I still have mine from the last mission," said Connor.

"Not like these you don't," replied Amir, excitedly handing them each a pair. "Put them on."

As Connor and Ling slipped on the shades, Amir closed the blinds and switched off the room's light, plunging them into darkness.

"Hey, I can't see a thing!" Ling exclaimed.

"Flick the switch on the right edge of the frame."

Finding the tiny switch with his fingernail, Connor gasped in awe as Amir and Ling reappeared before his eyes in a shimmering silver light. "Now, these are cool!"

"Night-vision sunglasses," explained Amir, enjoying the looks of astonishment on his friends' faces. "Cutting-edge nanotechnology in the lens allows you to see in the dark as if there's a full moon. There's a smart layer of nano-photonic film that converts infrared light to visible. Unlike standard night-vision goggles that amplify only visible light, these have the advantage of not being vulnerable to flaring when confronted with a bright light."

Amir switched on the main light to prove his point. Connor could still see perfectly well, even if the room before him appeared overexposed. He flicked off the night-vision mode, and everything returned to normal.

"What else is in your bag of tricks?" asked Ling, now caught up in the thrill of having such advanced gadgets at their disposal.

"Well, there's this," said Amir, handing Ling a large white bottle.

"What is it?" she asked eagerly. "A miniature life raft? A smoke grenade?"

"No, but it will protect you from the greatest danger you face on your mission."

Ling looked at him expectantly. "So, what is it?"

Amir was barely able to suppress his grin. "It's sunscreen."

17

"What's going on with your grades in math? You got As and Bs in your other subjects, but a C in math."

Connor groaned down the phone. "*Mum* . . . I've had a few other things on my mind recently."

"Like what?"

Connor didn't know how to answer that. His mother had no idea he was training and operating as a professional bodyguard. She'd been told that he was attending a boarding school for gifted and talented athletes, the cost sponsored by a special government scholarship program. That's why his mother received a report card only for the standard subjects. His appraisals in the other areas, ranging from world affairs to unarmed combat to anti-ambush training, went directly to Colonel Black.

"It's difficult to explain," he admitted.

"Oh . . ." she said, a knowing tone entering her voice. "You mean, a girl?"

Connor shifted awkwardly from one foot to the other and felt a flush fire his cheeks at her line of questioning. "No, nothing like that," he protested.

"Listen, you can't let girls distract you from your work," said his mother, ignoring his protest and thinking she knew better. "They'll cause you enough trouble when you're older."

Connor could think of two girls—Emily and Chloe—who *might* cause him trouble a lot sooner than that.

"Can we talk about something else?" he urged. "Like you. How are you doing?"

"Oh, really well, thanks," she replied cheerily. "Improving day by day with Sally's help."

Connor listened as she told him how her live-in caregiver had encouraged her to take vitamin D and do some light yoga exercises. This, along with a recent course of acupuncture, had really helped to ease her symptoms. However, all the while his mother talked, Connor could tell from the strain in her voice that she was putting on a brave front. As a sufferer of multiple sclerosis, she had difficulty with coordination and balance, was easily fatigued, and was often struck with numbness or grinding pain.

Her condition, along with his aging gran's needs, had been the primary reason for Connor agreeing to join Guardian. In return for his service, Colonel Black had offered a complete care package for his mum and gran. Such health support was way beyond the financial reach of an unemployed army widow like his mother. And, at the time of the offer, his family had already been struggling with basic day-to-day living costs. The colonel's deal was a virtual godsend. But as part of the deal, Connor couldn't reveal to her his true role. The highly secretive Guardian organization relied on the fact that few people knew of its existence, allowing teenagers like Connor to act as invisible defense shields for vulnerable and high-profile targets. Besides, his mother would probably be furious if she discovered he was following in his father's footsteps—a path that might easily lead him to an early grave too. He didn't like deceiving her about it one bit, but he *did* like seeing her cared for properly. It was a trade-off and one worth making.

"I'm really glad to hear things are improving," said Connor, despite his deeper concerns for her. "Listen, I'm calling to let you know that I'll be away on a sailing trip next month, so I might be out of contact for a bit."

During the school year, Connor religiously called home every week to check on his mother and gran, and he knew they both eagerly awaited his calls.

"A *sailing* trip! You certainly lead an exciting life at this new school of yours," remarked his mother. Connor heard her relay the news to his gran and Sally before returning to the phone. "One thing, son, please take extra care. I don't want you injuring yourself like last time."

"I will," said Connor, hoping the same himself. His mother

had been led to believe that he'd hurt his leg falling off a mountain bike, the pretense necessary to keep his involvement in Guardian confidential.

"Hold on, love, Sally's calling me, but your gran wants a word. We'll talk again when you get back."

There was a clatter as the phone changed hands. "How's my big man?"

"Fine, Gran. And you?"

"As fit as a fiddle and as right as rain," she replied brightly.

Connor laughed; that was what she always said.

His gran lowered her voice. "I know she won't have told you, but your mum may have to start using a wheelchair soon."

"What?" said Connor, stunned. "She said she was getting better."

"In some respects she is, and she doesn't want to worry you. Sally just recommended that your mum use one when she goes out. She's not as steady on her feet as she was."

"But Mum was fine when I saw you both last month."

His gran sighed. "She had a relapse last weekend."

Connor fell silent. This cruel disease was slowly stripping his mother of her quality of life. Every time he called or visited, it seemed like another little piece of her had been taken away. And there was nothing he, or anyone else, could do about it. He balled his hand into a fist and screwed his eyes shut, holding back the tears that threatened to come.

"As you would expect, she's not particularly happy about

the idea," continued his gran, "but Sally says your 'scholar-ship program' will cover the cost of the chair."

Connor managed a sad smile. He might not be able to stop his mother's deterioration, but at least he could provide the necessary care for her—as well as for his gran. His work as a guardian meant they would be in safe hands, even if he was putting himself in harm's way and spending a lot less time with them both. He now understood his father's di-lemma when he'd been alive.

"Are *you* all right, my dear?" asked his gran gently.

"Yeah," he replied, wiping a sleeve across his reddened eyes.

"I hear you're going on a sailing trip," she asked, changing the subject. "Anywhere nice?"

Connor realized her question was loaded. "The Seychelles."

"Ooh, lovely," she cooed. "Anything else you can tell me about your 'trip'?"

"Not really . . ." replied Connor, aware that he was break-ing security protocol just by telling her his destination.

Charley appeared around the corner and gave him the nod.

"Sorry, Gran, I have to go," said Connor. "Give Mum my love, and I'll see you both soon."

"Is that a promise?"

Connor momentarily hesitated. His gran's question was no mere platitude but a wish for a binding agreement. "Of course, Gran."

"Good. Then stay safe, my dear . . . stay safe."

Connor could hear the anxious crack in his gran's voice as she ended the call.

He hated putting her through such worry and often wondered whether he should ever have told her about Guardian in the first place. But his gran would have seen through his half-truths like a priest in a confessional. She was too sharp and had lived too long to be fooled by anyone, let alone her grandson. Besides, Connor trusted her and needed her. She was his rock and, when life got tough, the one person he could always turn to for advice.

"Everything okay at home?" asked Charley.

Connor looked up, suddenly aware he'd been staring off into space. "Yeah . . . My gran's fine. But my mum may have to use a wheelchair. She isn't looking forward to it."

"I know the feeling," said Charley, patting the armrest of her chair. "If your mother ever needs someone to talk to, I'd be happy to give her a call."

Connor smiled warmly at Charley's kindness. "Thanks, I'll let her know."

"Come on," said Charley, pivoting on the spot. "The car's waiting to take you to the airport."

Connor followed Charley out to the black Range Rover parked on the long sweeping drive of Guardian headquarters. The rest of Alpha team had assembled on the steps to see him and Ling off. Jody was in the driver's seat, checking the

GPS navigation for traffic, and Ling sat in the back, seat belt on, ready to go.

"Hurry up, partner!" she shouted, slapping the seat next to her. "Let's get this show on the road."

As Connor flung his bags into the back, Amir shouted, "Careful! That's my go-bag you're throwing around."

"It's mine now," replied Connor with a grin. "But I promise to look after it."

"You'd better," warned Amir, shaking his head in despair at the mishandling of his precious equipment.

"Good luck," called Marc, waving. Beside him, Richie offered a mock salute.

"Don't let Connor take all the glory, Ling," said Jason as Connor clambered in beside her.

Ling blew him a kiss. "Don't worry. He's carrying my bags!"

With a final thumbs-up to his teammates, Connor started to close the door, but Charley reached in and touched his arm.

"Try not to catch any bullets this time," she said.

Connor gave her a quizzical look. "Surely that's the point of a bodyguard."

Charley locked eyes with him. *"Only* if all else fails."

18

"Wake up, you lazy fish-eaters!"

The stern order in Somali barely roused the loose band of pirates who lay sprawled, like dozing lions, beneath the shade of the courtyard's single acacia tree. The blazing sun had baked the earth bone-dry, and the glaring white walls reflected the heat like mirrors. It was too hot even for the flies that buzzed listlessly in the still air.

"I said, GET UP! Oracle wants to see us," growled the towering man who strode over from the main building of the walled compound. With broad shoulders and rippling muscles, forged from a hard and brutal life, the man moved through the shimmering heat like a charging black rhino. A battle-worn AK-47 was slung over his shoulder.

"Hey, Spearhead, relax, man," said one of the pirates, chewing languidly on some khat leaves.

Spearhead ground his ivory-white teeth into a snarl and kicked the man in the ribs.

"Ow!" yelled the pirate, rolling away from the abuse.

"When I say move, Big Mouth, MOVE!"

The other men quickly got to their feet. Picking up their rifles, they grudgingly followed Spearhead across the blistering hot yard toward the main house. As they entered a dim, wide hallway, the harsh sun was left behind and the air became cool and welcoming. Leaving their weapons by the door, the pirate gang trudged barefoot into a spacious living room. An ornate crimson rug took center stage, framed by a slender beige divan. Thick maroon drapes blocked the persistent sunlight that tried to force its way through the barred windows. Each man instinctively salivated as their nostrils filled with the mouthwatering aroma of stewed goat's meat.

Oracle reclined on the rug against a gold-tasseled bolster, a wooden bowl of spiced ribs in one hand. In the other, he held a thin bone, which he gnawed on for the last vestiges of meat. Dressed in an olive-green shirt, with a red shawl slung over his right shoulder and a black diamond-pattern *ma'awis* around his hips, Oracle cut a princely figure compared with the unkempt appearance of his pirates. A pair of silver-mirrored aviator sunglasses were perched high on his closely shaved head. Behind him on the divan, within arm's reach, lay a loaded Browning semi-automatic pistol.

"Sit," said Oracle, picking with a fingernail at a bit of meat stuck between his teeth.

The pirates each found their spot on the luxurious rug and, squatting, waited mutely for their boss to finish his meal.

Eventually putting aside his empty bowl, Oracle licked his fingers, then wiped them on a square of white cotton cloth. "You'll be going to sea again within the week," he announced.

The pirates all looked at one another with a mix of excitement and trepidation.

"You've had another vision?" asked a rake-thin man with jug ears.

Oracle smiled enigmatically. "Well, let's say . . . I foresaw fortune headed our way." He patted the blue sports bag cradled at his side. "We have a new investor."

"What's happening with the cargo ship we've already got?" asked Spearhead.

"That'll take a few more months of negotiation," replied Oracle. "Red Claw and his men can handle the babysitting. I need *you* for the serious work."

"But what about boats?" asked Big Mouth. "We lost two skiffs in the last hijack."

"It's all in hand," reassured Oracle. "Four brand-new twin three-fifty-horsepower outboards are on their way from Dubai."

"Can I pilot one?" a skinny bucktoothed young pirate asked, beaming.

"When you can grow a beard, you can!" Spearhead said, laughing.

As other pirates joined in the laughter, a phone chirped loudly.

"It's not mine," said Big Mouth quickly, knowing how much their boss frowned on having his meetings interrupted.

The ring persisted, and now every pirate checked his phone, each one praying it wasn't his. Gradually all eyes turned to the innocuous sports bag.

Oracle's brow furrowed slightly. Then he nodded to Spearhead to investigate. The great man bent down, unzipped the bag and removed a brown envelope. Its contents rang and vibrated. Ripping the envelope open, he pulled out a slim cell phone.

Oracle indicated with a jut of his chin for Spearhead to answer.

"*Iska warran?*" Spearhead listened for a moment, then said, "It's for you, boss," offering the handset.

Oracle warily studied the intruding phone before putting it to his ear.

"*Haa* . . . Yes, I speak English . . ." he said, switching languages fluidly. "Not at all, I was just having lunch . . . It's always a pleasure to hear from an investor." However, his cordial words did not match his stony expression. "Yes, I've received the full amount . . ."

The other pirates looked on, bemused by the foreign

conversation. Only Spearhead among the pirate gang had a working command of English, and he listened with growing curiosity.

"Your request is highly unusual . . . What do you mean it *isn't* a request?" Oracle's expression darkened at the caller's unheard response. "I answer to *no one!*" he snapped. "No . . . I have not yet looked in the envelope."

Oracle waved an impatient hand at Spearhead to pass it over. As he turned out the contents, several typed sheets of paper and a large photo print of a yacht landed on the carpet. "Yes, I can see the target you propose. But why would you want *that* when I could get you an oil tanker?"

Oracle listened to his investor's reply, and his eyes took on a diamond-like sheen. "*How much* did you say?"

As the figure was reconfirmed, a greasy smile slid across Oracle's lips. "Then we are in business, my friend. I'll let you know as soon as my men are ready."

Oracle flipped shut the cell phone and laid it beside his handgun.

"Get Mr. Wi-Fi," he ordered.

Spearhead jerked his bald head at Big Mouth, who left the room and returned a moment later accompanied by a be-spectacled young man. With a neatly trimmed goatee, Ber-muda shorts and a blue New York Yankees T-shirt, Mr. Wi-Fi looked more like a university student than a hardened pirate. Under his arm he carried a battered laptop.

"We have a hijacking to plan," announced Oracle.

"About time," Mr. Wi-Fi said, smiling and opening his laptop, angling the screen so Oracle could see the live satellite image of the Gulf of Aden. "I'm tracking several high-value vessels as we speak."

"Forget about them," Oracle said, causing Mr. Wi-Fi's smile to vanish in dismay. He handed him the photo along with one of the info sheets. "*This* is our target."

Perching on the edge of the divan, Mr. Wi-Fi hunched over his whirring laptop. The pirates ostrich-necked to try to see what he was doing as his fingers rapidly danced across the keyboard. In the search window of a hacked Marine Intelligence Unit website, Mr. Wi-Fi typed *motor yacht* Orchid . . .

19

Maddox Sterling's office was a glass wonder. A capsule of 360-degree views, its four walls were constructed from electro-chromatic smart windows. The special glass, stretching from floor to ceiling, automatically altered its transparency according to the sun's strength and position in the sky. Being midmorning, the eastern wall had darkened to amber brown against the golden light streaming over Sydney's Central Business District.

Maddox Sterling, his back to the shaded sun, stood as Colonel Black, Ling and Connor were ushered in by his personal assistant. Entering the office was almost disconcerting. For Connor, it felt as if he could step right off the edge of the towering skyscraper and plummet fifty floors to the pavement below.

The office's interior design was as minimalist as the walls themselves. There was no furniture beyond a slim glass desk and four chrome-and-black-leather chairs. For a man in charge of a billion-dollar corporation, the see-through desk was strangely uncluttered. No paperwork, no computer monitor, no ornaments, not even a picture of his daughters— just an ultra-thin aluminum laptop and a cordless phone.

"Welcome to Sydney," said Maddox Sterling, greeting each of them with a firm handshake and a slick smile, then gesturing for them to take a seat.

"Thank you, Mr. Sterling," said Colonel Black, settling into one of the designer chairs, Ling and Connor taking their places on either side of him.

From behind his desk, Maddox Sterling swiveled toward an unbroken view of one of Sydney's most iconic landmarks. With a broad sweep of his hand as if he owned it, he declared, "Without doubt, the finest natural harbor in the world, made even more magnificent by our stunning opera house and the Sydney Harbor Bridge. Truly a sight to behold."

Connor stared out the window—first, at the sparkling waters of the harbor, then at the overlapping shell roof of the opera house, and finally at the dramatic latticework of arching girders that spanned the waterway. It certainly was an impressive sight.

"They call the bridge the Coathanger because of its arch-based design," Mr. Sterling explained, a hint of disapproval noticeable in his tone. "But that does it a great disservice. Up close, it's truly majestic. The arch soars so high, a ten-story building could pass beneath. And the weight of the bridge is monstrous. Over three hundred and fifty thousand tons of steel and six million rivets went into its construction."

He glanced sideways at Connor and Ling, checking to see that they were suitably impressed.

"The bridge has a surface area larger than sixty soccer pitches, which means it needs a fifty-man team working three hundred and sixty-five days a year just to clean and repaint it. Obviously such maintenance is incredibly dangerous work. That's why they've recently employed two autonomous robots for the more hazardous sections. An appropriate reduction of risk."

Mr. Sterling pivoted back to face them. His cobalt-blue eyes fixed first on Ling, then on Connor, with an intensity that seemed to cut right through them both.

"Similarly, I've employed *you two* to reduce the risk in my family's life."

Connor wasn't sure how he felt about being compared with a mindless robot, but Mr. Sterling didn't seem to consider this an insult and carried on regardless.

"I already have a personal protection officer, who will be accompanying me on the trip. My yacht has a ship security officer, and there are other safeguards in place here and at home. But, as you know, that wasn't enough. I have two beautiful daughters who are very precious to me. And God forbid I have a repeat of last year."

"You can rest assured, Mr. Sterling, that my guardians will protect your daughters," said Colonel Black. "Since this is a family vacation, their presence will appear to be relaxed and low profile. But I can guarantee they'll be on constant alert to any threat and avert any danger."

"Your organization comes highly recommended, Colonel Black, so I expect nothing less."

Colonel Black didn't flinch under Maddox's steely gaze. And he gave no answer, none being required when his belief in his recruits was absolute.

Mr. Sterling wagged a finger in Connor's direction. "Is this the boy who saved the US president's daughter's life?"

Colonel Black's eyes narrowed. "How did you know about that?"

"I have my sources. But don't be concerned, Colonel. Keeping your organization a secret is in my interests. So, is he?"

Colonel Black nodded.

"Then I want *him* protecting Emily."

Connor glanced over at Ling. Her lips had tightened, clearly taking the role assignment as an affront to her abilities. But she stayed silent.

"Not a problem," agreed the colonel. "Now, I understand that you—"

A knock at the door disturbed them, and Mr. Sterling's assistant appeared. "Sorry to interrupt, but the editor in chief says this can't wait."

Mr. Sterling nodded his assent, and a redheaded woman in a tailored pinstripe jacket-and-skirt suit entered.

"What is it, Ruth?"

She shot a doubtful glance at the colonel and two young teenagers in his office. "This might be better in private."

"My apologies, Colonel Black," said Mr. Sterling with a regretful smile, "but the world rarely stops in my line of business."

"We understand," said Colonel Black, rising to his feet. "I can communicate any outstanding queries via your assistant."

"Then I'll bid you farewell and look forward to seeing these two in the Seychelles," said Mr. Sterling, offering both Ling and Connor a courteous nod. "But before then I've arranged for you to meet my daughters for lunch at one of my restaurants. My assistant has the details."

Ruth stepped aside to allow them out through the glass door. As the door slowly closed behind them, Connor overheard a familiar name.

"There's more to Harry Gibb's heart attack than meets the eye . . ." the editor in chief began. ". . . speculation he was murdered."

"What evidence do you have?" asked Mr. Sterling.

"Nothing conclusive at the moment. But I may have a source."

"Okay, look into it. If it's true, it'll take the heat off the *Daily* for allegedly causing that idiot's death through stress. As well as help sell a bucketload more papers—"

Then the glass door slid shut.

20

"Is this a *joke*?" said Emily, putting down her glass of lemonade hard enough to make the ice tinkle. She stared at Connor and Ling as if waiting for the punch line.

Sitting in a rooftop restaurant overlooking the golden-sanded curve of Manly Beach, Connor removed his sunglasses and shook his head in response. "Not at all. We've been assigned as your guardians."

He looked from Emily to Chloe, a mirror image of her sister, with what he hoped was a convincing and reassuring smile. Both the girls wore pale yellow summer dresses and matching designer sunglasses, flipped back on their heads to keep their straw-blond hair out of their eyes. The twins had ordered the same tuna salad and tall iced lemonades.

Chloe maintained her composure, while Emily gave an incredulous snort. "*Guardians?*" she said, and laughed.

When her sister didn't join in her laughter, Emily spun on her, eyes narrowing with suspicion. "Did you know about this?"

Chloe started to open her mouth, but Emily had already read her expression. "Typical!" she cried, picking up her fork and waving it at her sister. "Daddy tells you everything."

Chloe sighed. "He didn't want you to flip out, thinking that he was being overprotective."

"*Overprotective?* When has he been around us long enough to even *be* protective!" Emily stabbed at her tuna salad with the fork. "Well, it's blindingly obvious just how much Daddy values our lives if he isn't even hiring a real bodyguard."

Chloe offered a rueful smile to Connor and Ling. "Sorry," she said, then mouthed, *Not a good day,* and raised an eyebrow meaningfully. Connor, recalling the psychological report detailing Emily's mood swings, nodded in understanding.

"But I do have to agree with my sister," continued Chloe, her tone hardening. "You're not what I expected. You don't really look like bodyguards."

"We're not supposed to," said Connor. "We act as low-profile, invisible protection. That makes you less of a target when we're out and about."

Chloe gave Ling the once-over, clearly unimpressed. "You aren't exactly very big or strong. How on earth can you protect us?"

"I'm a black belt in martial arts," Ling replied coolly. "So is Connor."

"*Really?*" said Emily, her tone dripping with sarcasm. "Can you catch a fly with a pair of chopsticks like the Karate Kid?"

Connor noticed Ling's fingers clench around her glass of iced tea as she struggled to control her rising irritation with the girl. He shot her a silent warning to chill out. Taking a deep breath, Ling managed a strained smile. "No, but I do know how to bring down a fully grown man by kicking him in the—"

"They get the point," Connor interrupted, holding up a hand and wishing now that Colonel Black hadn't gone back to the hotel. He turned to the sisters. "Look, I realize that we're not your stereotypical bodyguards. But we *are* fully trained in unarmed combat, surveillance and threat assessments."

"I feel safer already!" muttered Emily.

"And we have experience in protecting people like you," Connor persisted.

Chloe raised a dubious eyebrow. "Like who?"

Connor replied with a regretful shrug. "Unfortunately, we can't tell you. It would break client confidentiality."

"So . . ." said Chloe after a moment's serious thought, "you're asking us to trust *you* with our lives."

"Absolutely," Connor replied with as much confidence as he could convey.

"I don't *think* so," said Emily, wielding her fork at them like it was a weapon. "The last time I trusted someone I didn't know, I ended up in a hellhole!"

21

An uncomfortable silence hung over the table, Chloe trying to make eye contact with her sister while Ling and Connor fidgeted with their drinks. Connor wanted to offer his sympathy, but there was little that could be said in response to Emily's outburst without sounding trite or insensitive.

After a few minutes of pushing their salads around their plates, Chloe sighed and piped up, "Listen, Emily, Daddy's made his decision. They'll be with us on the yacht whether we like it or not, so we might as well try to get along. And why not take advantage of their supposed protection? Let's go down to the beach. We haven't been allowed that much freedom in months!"

Emily pushed her plate away and put aside her napkin. "Fine," she said, offering Connor and Ling a civil smile. "At least my father will have someone to blame this time when things go wrong."

Connor tried not to react to Emily's bad attitude. Instead,

he returned her smile and replied good-naturedly, "With us on board, it should all be smooth sailing."

"Ha, ha," said Emily without humor as she picked up her Gucci handbag and strode off.

Shouldering a matching leather handbag, Chloe joined her sister and headed for the stairs.

"Well, that was a pleasant lunch," said Ling, turning to Connor with a forced smile. "Can't wait for the trip!"

Connor sighed at the thought. "They just need time to get used to the idea."

"Well, I'm sure glad Emily's *your* responsibility," said Ling, rising from her chair.

"So much for team spirit!"

"Hey, you're the hotshot bodyguard," she replied, punching him playfully on the arm. "You can handle her."

Connor just hoped he could. An uncooperative Principal made the task of being an effective bodyguard almost impossible. "Then we'll just have to convince them both that we can do the job."

Catching up with the twins at the restaurant entrance, Connor quickened his pace to reach the glass double doors first. Stepping outside and holding the door, he did a quick scan up and down the road. Although Operation Gemini hadn't officially started, he nonetheless assumed his bodyguard role. So did Ling, who hung back inside the café to cover their backs.

In his split-second surveillance sweep, Connor observed a couple of cars heading in their direction and a battered white pickup truck parked on the opposite side. Farther along the street a woman was pushing a stroller with a screaming baby inside, while nearby a young couple was entering a clothing store. Satisfied that none of them presented a viable threat, Connor stepped aside to allow Emily and Chloe out.

"Thank you," said Chloe, taking Connor's door-holding as a gesture of politeness rather than security.

"Just making sure the coast was clear," Connor explained.

She glanced over the road at the turquoise sea and white-crested waves peeling along the shoreline. "Of course it is!" She laughed, donning her sunglasses. "It's a glorious day."

"You misunderstand," said Ling. "Connor was performing a security sweep before you left the restaurant."

Chloe raised an eyebrow. "Manly Beach is *hardly* a war zone."

"You'd be surprised," said Connor as they crossed the road to the wide tree-lined promenade that hugged the golden stretch of beach. Passing by a bench, Connor noticed the eyes of four teenage surfers keenly following their progress. But he wasn't overly concerned. Emily and Chloe's twin looks naturally attracted attention—though Connor realized that at some point they were bound to draw *unwanted* attention.

"There may not be guns or bombs going off around here," he explained, "but you're still at risk."

"From what?" asked Chloe, gesturing with her hand at the idyllic scene—the path thronged with laughing teenagers, sun worshippers, red-faced tourists and bronzed surfers, their boards tucked under their arms. A leisurely stream of bikes glided by in the bicycling lane, while roller skaters weaved in and out at high speed.

"You're not only at risk from known threats, such as enemies of your father or professional kidnappers," Ling replied, glancing meaningfully at Emily, "but also from anything that might happen on the street—muggings, pickpocketing, car accidents, trip hazards, fights—"

"You're beginning to sound like our father. We're only going for a *walk* along the beach," said Chloe, sighing in exasperation.

"That's when a Principal like you is most vulnerable," Connor said. "See that woman over there?" He pointed to a woman in a red bikini spread out on a beach towel, chatting on her phone and gazing at the surf. "She's in Code White."

"Code *what*?" asked Emily, showing her first sign of interest in the conversation.

"Code White. It refers to a person's mental state when they're not tuned in to their environment, lost in their own bubble. Most people live their lives like that: oblivious to the potential dangers surrounding them. Even from here I can see that her bag contains her wallet, car keys and an iPad. Someone could rob her before she's even aware that her belongings are gone."

"Aren't you being a bit paranoid?" Chloe suggested.

"No, just hypervigilant," replied Ling. "As your guardians, we can't afford to space out like that. We need to be in Code Yellow—relaxed awareness—the default mind-set of a trained bodyguard."

"So you're constantly on edge?" said Emily, her curiosity overcoming her mood.

"Not exactly," replied Connor. "We're just aware of the people around us, the environment we're walking through and any potential dangers. For example, did either of you notice the white pickup truck parked on the other side of the road earlier?"

"No," said Chloe, looking back over her shoulder.

"Then you wouldn't have seen the two guys in the front seats."

Chloe and Emily turned to stare.

"So what?" said Chloe. "They're just hanging out."

"If that's the case, why do they have a pair of high-powered binoculars on the dashboard?" Connor challenged.

Chloe shrugged. "Maybe they're checking out the waves?"

"Or they're bird-watchers," suggested Emily, nodding up toward the branches of the pine trees where a couple of white cockatoos squawked loudly.

"With bandanas and tinted sunglasses, they don't strike

me as the type to watch that sort of birdlife. And, with no boards in the back, they aren't here to surf."

"So what *are* they doing?" asked Chloe, an edge of excitement entering her voice.

"I've no proof they're a threat," said Connor. "They could be undercover police officers on surveillance. Or simply workmen on their lunch break. I only *suspect* they might be bag thieves. But since I'm alert to their presence, they can't take me by surprise, like they would that woman."

"Wow! I didn't realize there was so much to this bodyguard business," said Chloe, studying Connor and Ling in a new light.

"That's barely scratching the surface of what we do," replied Ling, shooting Connor a sly wink that at least Chloe was beginning to appreciate their worth. "But, if people were more aware, they'd be less likely to get into trouble. Who knows, if either of you or your father had been more tuned in last year, the kidnapping might not even have happened."

Connor winced at Ling's tactlessness.

"Well, it did," said Chloe, glaring at Ling as Emily's expression darkened and she once more fell into tight-lipped silence. "Anyway, you don't know what happened, so you have no right to pass judgment."

"I'm only saying ... that it won't happen this time because you've got *us* to watch out for you," blurted Ling, trying to rescue the situation.

Chloe's phone rang, a pop song ringtone interrupting the tense moment. Chloe pulled out a slim white phone and answered. "Hi, Josie . . . Yeah, okay . . . Just down on Manly . . . I know, it's been *forever* . . . Yeah, I'd love to, but you know what my father's like . . . You could come over to ours . . ."

As Chloe chatted with her friend, she slowed to a stop by the sea wall. But Emily kept going—splitting the group up. Ling hung behind, giving Chloe the space to talk, while Connor stuck with his Principal, purposefully maneuvering himself to her right-hand side. During close-protection "walking drills," he'd learned that this position was best for a right-handed bodyguard. In an attack, he could pull the Principal away with his left hand while using his stronger right arm to fend off the attacker or draw a weapon.

As they wandered away, Ling held open her palms in a sign of sheepish apology to Connor. But he just waved the problem aside. Mistakes happened.

Now that he was on his own with Emily, Connor decided it was an opportunity to try to bond with her. "Sorry about what Ling said back there," he began. "She can be quite . . . *blunt* at times."

"Hmm," said Emily, barely acknowledging him, her mind seemingly elsewhere.

"Perhaps it would help if you told me what did happen."

"I'd prefer not to talk about it."

"Sure," said Connor.

After a couple more attempts at conversation, both of which resulted in monosyllabic replies, he decided the best strategy would be to walk in silence. No point in annoying Emily further. Besides, it wasn't his job to be her friend. He was there to protect her.

Connor maintained a sharp watch on his surroundings. A couple of Rollerbladers were speeding along on the path ahead. A pair of rainbow lorikeets screeched in the branches above. A blond surfer with his board tucked under his arm strutted past. He gave Emily the eye until he noticed Connor staring at him.

As they strolled along the shaded avenue of towering pine trees, Emily studied Connor out of the corner of her eye.

"Why do you keep looking up?" she asked eventually.

Connor, who hadn't realized he was being so obvious, replied, "Dropbears."

Emily did a double take, then let out a short burst of laughter—her first genuine expression of good humor.

Connor furrowed his brow. "What's so funny?"

"You are," she replied. "Dropbears of all things!"

"But my Aussie friend Jason said they were really vicious."

Emily searched Connor's face and saw only genuine concern, which made her laugh even harder. "You actually think they're *real*. It's just a joke Aussies tell tourists to scare or confuse them. You Brits are so gullible!"

Connor felt his face flush. He'd been suckered by Jason's dropbear story. And now he looked like a fool in front of his Principal. This was not a good start to the operation. Emily would think he was a total idiot.

He was snapped out of his thoughts when Emily's laughter suddenly turned to a scream.

22

The attack happened so fast—and so unexpectedly—that for a split second Connor failed to react . . .

Then his bodyguard training took over. Seizing Emily's shoulder with his left hand, he wrenched her away from the threat and stepped forward to shield her with his body.

The Rollerblader was a blur as he barreled into Connor. The man grabbed Emily's Gucci bag and attempted to rip it from her shoulder. His forward momentum spun Connor and Emily around, almost pulling them off their feet.

In an effort to break the Rollerblader's fierce grip, Connor drove his knuckled fist into the tendons of the man's wrist. The man, a bare-chested brute with a roaring lion tattoo on his right bicep, grunted in pain but hung on tenaciously. Spinning them around again, he caught Connor across the jaw with his elbow. Connor's head rocked back, and he tasted blood. The Rollerblader yanked at the bag, and the strap snapped. Emily tumbled to the ground, Connor sprawling on top of her.

"Are you . . . all right?" Connor gasped as he watched the mugger skate away, his loot in tow.

She nodded, then stuttered, "M-my bag . . ."

But the high-speed thief didn't get far.

Ling, who'd witnessed the attack from a distance, snatched a board from a passing surfer and swung it hard at the escaping thief. The edge slammed with full force into the man's gut. A pained exhalation burst from his lungs, and he lost his grip on the bag. Nose-diving into the concrete, the skater careered across the path and into a nearby tree trunk.

But no sooner had Ling dealt with this attacker than a second Rollerblader charged in Chloe's direction.

"Watch out!" Connor bawled at the top of his lungs. But Chloe just stood there, wide-eyed, like a rabbit caught in the headlights.

The Rollerblader, a dome-headed black man with wrap-around sunglasses, sped toward her with the force of a battering ram. With only seconds to react, Ling discarded the surfboard and launched herself into his path. Small as she was, she collided hard enough to knock him off course. They both struck the concrete sea wall and toppled over the side. Pile-driving into the sand below and crushing a child's sand castle, Ling and the Rollerblader fought to disentangle themselves.

Meanwhile, Connor rushed over with Emily to her sister in readiness to protect them *both* if he had to.

"Stay close to me," he ordered the girls as Ling and the second Rollerblader battled it out on the beach.

Wrestling in his grip, Ling flipped her head back, catching the skater under the chin. His teeth rattled in his skull, and he roared in fury. Shoving a large hand into Ling's face, he pushed her away, rolled on top and used his weight to crush her. Ling was pinned, but Connor couldn't go to her rescue. If he did, he'd be leaving both their Principals unprotected.

He shouldn't have worried, though. As the man attempted to subdue her, Ling reached down and pinched a nerve point in the middle of his inner thigh. He yelped like a kicked dog and leaped off Ling as if he'd been electrocuted.

"Leave me alone, you wildcat!" he shouted, shocked by her combat abilities.

As Ling flipped to her feet and advanced on him, he snatched in desperation at a handful of sand and threw it into her face. Too close to avoid the attack, Ling staggered away, half blinded. By the time she'd wiped the grit from her eyes, the Rollerblader had stumbled along the beach and up the steps to the boulevard.

Stunned beachgoers stared at the four teenagers, trying to make sense of what had just happened.

"Are you okay?" Connor called to Ling.

"Yes," she replied, still spitting sand. "Are the twins safe?"

Still buzzing with adrenaline, Connor scanned the area for further threats. Just because they'd fended off this attack didn't mean the danger was over.

"Yes, it seems all clear."

The lifeguard was sprinting over, calling the police on his walkie-talkie. A group of beach bums were applauding Ling's fighting skills as she made her way up the steps. The blond surfer near Chloe was kneeling beside his board, checking it for damage.

But the two Rollerbladers had vanished.

So too had the white pickup truck.

23

"That was no random mugging," said Connor, nursing his lip with a bag of ice from the hotel's minibar. Having called Mr. Sterling's chauffeur, they'd escorted the girls back to their home, a gated mansion on Point Piper. Then the two of them had been dropped off at their hotel in Circular Quay.

"Thieves often work in pairs," Ling observed as she settled back on her bed and flicked through the TV channels.

"Don't you think it's a little suspicious that *both* the girls were attacked?"

Ling shrugged. "Not really. They were carrying expensive designer handbags. That made them targets. Hey, cool, a Bruce Lee movie!" She tossed aside the remote.

Connor set down his bag of ice. "How can you be so relaxed about all of this?"

"We stopped them. Job done," said Ling, folding her arms

behind her head and focusing on the TV screen. "Now stop worrying and watch the movie."

"I disagree. There's *everything* to be worried about. It can't be coincidence. The attack had to be planned. What about those men in the pickup truck? Perhaps my instinct was right. Maybe they were carrying out surveillance on us."

Ling glanced over. "For what purpose?"

"To test our skills."

Ling sat up and muted the TV. "Are you suggesting that Mr. Sterling would have his own daughters *mugged*?"

Connor nodded. "Either that or someone else has a personal grudge against the girls. If it's the latter, then we have a real problem on our hands."

There was a knock at the door. Connor got up, checked the peephole, then unlocked the latch.

Colonel Black strode in and turned off the TV. "I just got off the phone with Mr. Sterling."

Connor braced himself for the fallout. Although they'd protected the girls, he knew he'd been slow to react. That stupid dropbear prank of Jason's had distracted him at the crucial moment. If he'd been tuned in and in Code Yellow, he would have noticed the Rollerblader's approach, questioned his diversion from the bike path and taken action to remove Emily from the danger zone *before* the attack. Only Ling's speedy intervention had kept the Rollerblader from escaping with her bag.

"So what did he say?" Ling prompted.

Colonel Black offered one of his rare smiles. "He was delighted with your reactions today."

Relieved, Connor slammed a fist into his palm. "I told you!"

The colonel's brow knotted with puzzlement. "What are you talking about?"

Connor explained his suspicions about the mugging being a setup job.

Colonel Black glanced out the hotel window at the opera house and rubbed his chin. "You have no firm proof. And, judging by my conversation with Mr. Sterling, I'd be surprised. So we must assume a hostile party is involved. Could you identify the men?"

"Yes. Mine had a distinctive lion tattoo on his arm," replied Connor.

"And I won't easily forget how bad my guy's breath smelled!" said Ling, waving a hand in front of her pinched nose.

"But the men in the truck, no," Connor admitted. "Their bandanas and shades covered most of their faces."

"Then this is our wake-up call," said Colonel Black, fixing them with his flint-gray eyes. "Operation Gemini has to be watertight. In the Seychelles, you'll be surrounded by sunscreen and bikinis, but you must remain focused on the job. Remember, you are *not* on vacation."

24

Mr. Wi-Fi whistled in admiration as he examined the *Orchid*'s specifications online. "This is one fine yacht: one hundred and fifty feet of pure French style and craftsmanship."

He scrolled down the page, his small rounded eyes sucking in the information.

"Four decks, six guest cabins, a range of four thousand nautical miles, cruising speed of *twenty-four knots*." He glanced over the rim of his glasses at the mighty bulk of Spearhead. "That's fast for its size! Carbon-reinforced hull and superstructure, hot tub, sauna, gymnasium, speedboat, Jet Skis—"

"Just give me the weaknesses," ordered the pirate, who sat cross-legged beside the computer whiz in Oracle's makeshift operations room. No more than a whitewashed concrete box, the airless room had a red tiled floor, two barred windows and a bare electric lightbulb that hung from the cracked ceiling like a withered fruit. The bulb flickered, a slave to the fluctuating output of the compound's generator, and its pale yellow light dimmed over the two plotting men.

Mr. Wi-Fi sucked his teeth thoughtfully. "Well, her top speed is twenty-eight knots. That means your boats will be hard-pressed to outrun her. You'll need to sneak up in the blind spot of their radar"—he indicated the rear of the vessel on the laptop screen—"to have any hope of getting the jump on them."

"Leave the battle tactics to me," grunted Spearhead. "What's the height to the deck?"

Checking the boat's dimensions, Mr. Wi-Fi frowned. "The freeboard is quite high for a yacht, over fifteen feet. That might cause some probl—"

"Pah!" Spearhead dismissed, swatting at a mosquito on his neck. "I've scaled far higher. No problem."

"Still, I'd advise taking the *Orchid* from the stern," said Mr. Wi-Fi, angling the screen for the pirate to get a better view of the yacht. "See where the hull slopes over the tender garage? That's her weakest point."

Spearhead nodded, his marble-smooth brow shining in the glow of the buzzing lightbulb. "How many crew?"

"Ten," replied Mr. Wi-Fi, pulling up an internal layout of the boat. "Their quarters are in the bow on the lower deck. The bridge is on the upper deck. This plan doesn't show a citadel, but I'm guessing the best location for a safe room will be either the crew's quarters here"—he pointed to an area in the bow—"or the master cabin on the main deck. The yacht's equipped with a satellite Global Maritime Distress and Safety System, DSC radio and EPIRB, so you'll have to ensure all of those are disabled as soon as you board."

Spearhead snorted. "Shame we can't sabotage them beforehand. What about defenses?"

Mr. Wi-Fi laughed. "It's a *pleasure* boat, Spearhead. No razor wire or water cannon. You won't be impressing us with your war stories this time."

"Where's the challenge, then?" he said with a sly grin, his teeth appearing like a crescent moon in the twilight.

Mr. Wi-Fi peered over his glasses and replied, "There isn't any. Compared with a cargo ship, the *Orchid's* a sitting duck."

25

As Connor and Ling stepped from the gangplank onto the main deck of the super-yacht, a portly gentleman in a crisp white short-sleeved shirt with gold insignia, navy-blue trousers and a peaked white cap greeted them.

"Welcome aboard the *Orchid*. I'm Captain Thomas Locke," he said, tipping his cap respectfully at Ling. "This here is my chief officer, Danny Fielding."

A large bearded sailor with a tanned face, wrinkled by sun and salt water, saluted in greeting. "A pleasure to meet you," he said in a deep, gravelly tone.

The captain gestured toward the third man who completed the welcoming party on deck. "And this is Brad Harding, our ship security officer."

Tall with a sharp crew cut, Brad appeared every inch the textbook security officer. He possessed a well-honed physique that threatened to split the seams of his white polo shirt. With his anvil-like jaw, he looked as if he could chew through steel. When he offered a calloused hand to shake, Connor all too easily felt the iron strength in the man's grip.

"I've never worked with nippers before," said Brad, his Australian twang prominent as he beamed a lopsided smile, "but I expect we'll get on famously."

Connor and Ling smiled back, a little in awe of the man's sheer physical presence. "I'm sure we will," said Ling.

"You'll be reporting to Brad while on board," Captain Locke explained. "He's fully briefed me about your 'purpose' on my ship." His tone hardened slightly. "But as captain I have *ultimate* authority over all matters of safety and security. If you see something suspicious or there is a security breach of any sort, you're to report it immediately to either Brad or myself. I do *not* want you operating on your own. Do you understand?"

Connor exchanged a glance with Ling, both aware they'd need to report any such incidents to Colonel Black and Alpha team too.

"Yes, Captain," he replied, the correct form of address seeming to allay Captain Locke's concern.

"Good. Then I expect Mr. Sterling's vacation to go smoothly," he said with a satisfied nod. "The rest of the crew, whom you'll meet tomorrow, aren't aware of your credentials. They've been told you're special guests of Mr. Sterling's. I think this is best to maintain your cover and your security function."

"That's how we prefer to operate," said Ling.

Captain Locke tipped his cap again. "Then I'll leave you in Brad's capable hands."

The captain and his chief officer strode off toward a flight of steps leading to the bridge.

"I guess you must have had a long flight," said Brad, nodding at their crumpled clothes and washed-out faces.

"Twenty-seven hours and three flight changes, to be exact," replied Ling wearily. Dark shadows ringed her eyes, not surprising given the fact she'd binge-watched movies and only catnapped. Connor had barely slept either, the mysterious double mugging still preying on his mind.

"Well, I'll just give you a brief tour of the yacht before showing you to your quarters."

Picking up their bags, Connor and Ling followed Brad across the expansive aft deck. He opened a set of bay doors, and they exchanged the balmy warmth of the tropics for the cool interior of a large salon.

"This is the main living area," explained Brad as Connor and Ling stared openmouthed at the luxurious decor. White leather couches with lemon-zest scattered cushions took center stage around a low-slung coffee table. At the far end, a white-oak dining table was complemented by a mirrored cocktail bar. Floor-to-ceiling windows on either side let in reams of natural light while offering unbroken views of the Indian Ocean to port and, to starboard, the leisurely comings and goings of the island's main harbor.

"That's some view!" gushed Ling, peering through the window at the mist-shrouded peaks of Mahé's mountains, their lush forested slopes seeming to tumble into the glassy waters of the bay.

"But isn't this lounge a little *exposed*?" Connor observed, his bodyguard brain noting the security flaw.

Brad arched a wiry eyebrow at him. "Not bad observation skills, nipper, considering your jet lag. But these are smart windows. Mr. Sterling has a thing for them. Flick of a switch and they become obscure."

Reaching over to a wall panel, Brad pressed a button and the windows instantly turned white.

"Cool," said Ling.

Brad ushered Connor and Ling into a large hallway with a curving staircase, one flight leading up, another heading down.

"On this main deck, we also have a galley, study, cabin for Mr. Sterling's personal bodyguard and, up front"—Brad opened a sleek wooden door—"Mr. Sterling's personal master suite."

He stepped aside to allow them a peek into a spacious leather-upholstered bedroom. A wide panoramic window offered a captain's-eye view of the ocean from the comfort of a king-sized bed. As Connor and Ling tried to take in the sheer opulence of the room, Brad continued his tour. "On the upper deck is the sky lounge, a VIP guest room, the captain's cabin and the bridge. Above that is the sundeck with another bar, beach chairs and a hot tub."

"It's like a five-star hotel!" Ling gasped, unable to believe her eyes or ears.

"For Mr. Sterling and his guests, it certainly is," Brad replied, winking at her. "But it's a little more cramped in the crew's quarters."

"And that's where we're staying?" asked Connor.

Brad laughed. "No, you lucky dogs! For security reasons I've kept you close to the girls." He directed them down the curving staircase to the lower deck. "Emily's and Chloe's rooms are just down the corridor from you. These are your cabins."

He opened a pair of adjacent doors, revealing two well-appointed rooms with low futon-style beds. One was decorated in shades of olive green, the other decked out in rich chocolate brown.

"Now unpack, freshen up and get some shut-eye," instructed Brad. "I'll introduce you to the crew later. Then we'll start your MARSEC training in the morning."

"MARSEC?" queried Connor.

"Maritime Security. Meet me on the upper deck at 0700 hours."

He gave them a cheery nod, then bounded back up the staircase.

"I call this room," said Ling, tossing her pack onto the neatly pressed olive linen of her chosen bed. She explored the en-suite shower room, a gleaming cubicle of mirror and glass, and then, on inspecting the built-in designer wardrobes, was delighted to discover a concealed TV screen behind one panel. Throwing herself onto the bed, she gazed out the large porthole window. Through the glass, the topaz tropical waters rippled in the golden sunlight, and the fronds of palm trees could be seen swaying along a pure white beach.

"This is paradise," she cooed, glancing over her shoulder at Connor. "I know what the colonel said, but how can this assignment be anything *but* a vacation?"

26

"When it comes to maritime security matters, this isn't just the same as land that's blue," said Brad, indicating the turquoise sea lapping around them. "You need to acquire special skills and adopt a completely different mind-set."

Connor and Ling listened as they ate their breakfast in the sky lounge. The chef, a jolly man with a reassuringly large belly, had prepared them a delicious platter of watermelon, pineapple, kiwi and strawberries, along with honeyed Greek yogurt, granola and freshly squeezed orange juice.

The morning sun, shimmering in a cloudless sky, was wonderfully warming on Connor's back, and he felt more at ease than he had for a long while. Perhaps it was the combination of a good night's sleep, the idyllic surroundings and Brad's easy confidence that reassured him the operation would go smoothly.

Ling appeared even more laid-back and at one with the yachting lifestyle. Wearing her sunglasses, a bikini top and shorts, she looked ready for a day of sunbathing on the beach. But any sense of vacation spirit was soon quashed by the training itinerary laid out by Brad on the table.

"We have only a week before Mr. Sterling's arrival. So we have a lot to cover in very little time," he explained, pointing to the first day of the schedule. "You need to be able to handle the powerboat, read radar, understand charts, learn open-water survival techniques, be familiar with the ship security plan, operate the VHF radio—"

"We know how to do that already," said Ling, popping a fresh strawberry into her mouth.

"Stellar!" he said, grinning. "Then *you* can show me later, Lightning Ling."

Ling sat up. "How do you know my nickname?"

Brad tapped his nose confidentially with his index finger. "I do my research. Now finish your brekkie and follow me."

Leading them up to the sundeck, he stood by the gleaming rail and with a wide sweep of his arm gestured at the almost 360-degree outlook. Connor was once again struck by the majestic beauty of the island: all lush, forested slopes, coconut palms and colorful tropical birds, their gleeful chatter filling the scented air. And, judging by the number of other yachts and sailboats moored in the harbor, this slice of Eden attracted the super-rich like bees to a pot of honey.

"Vigilance is the key to protection on board a boat," Brad explained. "A constant watch is needed, both at sea and in anchorage. Don't rely on the crew to do any security detail; they're fully engaged in their normal crew duties."

Leaning against the rail, he pointed down at one of the deckhands, a lanky South African named Jordan, who was mopping the main deck while listening to music on his headphones.

"When in safe harbor, the crew are generally relaxed and unobservant, but *we* can't afford to be." He jerked his chin in the direction of a rubber dinghy buzzing by. "Small craft like that tender are scooting around all the time, so the approach of a suspect boat can go unnoticed. In a popular harbor like this, anyone with criminal intent has lots of useful cover, and it's even harder to spot them at night. That's why gangplanks should be raised whenever possible."

He glanced down at the *Orchid's* lowered gangway and clicked his tongue in irritation.

"In practical terms, the need for shore access means this happens only late at night. The problem is that harbor areas attract thieves and other lowlifes. So suspect *anyone* approaching our yacht, even officials in uniform. Don't be afraid to question them. Deception is a common tactic of the criminal. I've known ruses that range from people masquerading as pier-side pizza delivery boys to parading a pretty girl in a bikini as a distraction. Not that I've fallen for that one, of course."

He shot Connor a sly wink, then beckoned them both to

follow him back down the stairs and along a short corridor. Brad knocked on an open bulkhead door.

"Request permission to come on the bridge, Captain."

"Request granted," replied Captain Locke.

As they entered, Captain Locke nodded a brief greeting in their direction, then returned to the ship's systems check with Chief Officer Fielding.

The bridge wasn't anything like Connor had envisioned. Gone were the traditional wooden steering wheel for the helmsman, the brass compass tower and the table spilling over with paper charts. Instead, this super-yacht's bridge was decked out with computer monitors, dynamic positioning systems, integrated communication units, electronic radar displays, and a sports-car-style steering wheel and throttle, complete with leather-upholstered captain's chair.

"It's like the starship *Enterprise*," remarked Connor.

The chief officer grunted a laugh. "That's why you need a master's degree in computing just to pilot her."

"You don't say," said Ling as she stared, perplexed, at a screen of concentric circles, bearings and electronic waves and blips.

"That's the radar display," explained Brad. "Later I'll take you through the basics on how to read it, but the radar's main function is to detect land or other vessels. From a security point of view, it's the vessels we're interested in. If tuned correctly, the radar can give us early warning of a possible attack. See that blip there?" Brad indicated a green dot, then pointed out the window. "It's that fishing boat coming into harbor."

Connor and Ling looked out to sea and spotted the trawler approaching. Another, smaller dinghy with an outboard was crossing its path.

"Where's that boat on the radar?" asked Connor, checking the display.

"Ah, that's the problem with radar. It has limitations," replied Brad. "Small craft like that are often missed or appear as haphazard blips. If the sea is choppy, that degrades the radar's operation further. And if the pilot of the boat steers in a zigzag pattern, they become even more difficult to detect. On top of all that, you've got the radar's infamous blind spot directly to the stern of this yacht. For those reasons, when at sea, there must be someone on watch 24/7."

Brad looked at them both. "Remember, when it comes to detecting a threat at sea"—he pulled at his lower eyelid with a fingertip—"the Mark One eyeball is always the best defense."

27

The *Orchid*'s tender, a seven-meter luxury launch with 260-horsepower stern drive, powered across the bay, leaving a foaming wake in its trail. As Ling opened up the throttle, the wind whipped through Connor's tousled brown hair, and he had to grip the armrest for balance.

"Steady as she goes," said Brad, keeping a careful watch for other craft in their vicinity. "She's not a racing car."

But, judging by the grin plastered across Ling's face, she clearly thought it was. Connor had already received full instruction on how to start, steer and dock the tender. Now it was Ling's turn to get some practice. As she swung the boat around for another run, she hit an unexpected wave, and Connor was bounced out of his seat so hard that he tumbled over the side.

"MAN OVERBOARD!" Brad shouted as Connor hit the water, skipped once across its surface, then plunged beneath.

The sea, warm as it was, still shocked Connor's system,

and the rushing thunder of water in his ears and eyes momentarily disoriented him. Brad had warned them both that any man-overboard situation was potentially fatal. Drowning, exposure, hypothermia and impact injury were all very real risks, especially if the person wasn't wearing a life jacket. Fortunately, Connor was, and he rapidly floated back to the surface. By the time his head cleared the water, Ling had cut back on the throttle and was starting to make a controlled turn toward him.

As the tender approached, Ling tried to keep a fix on his location. He'd already drifted farther out to sea with the current, and it would be easy to lose sight of a head bobbing in the water, even in a little swell.

"Slow down," Brad warned Ling. "You're approaching too fast."

Ling cut back on the throttle, but it was too little too late.

"Careful!" said Brad. "You're going to run over him."

Ling tried to correct the tender's direction, but without enough power, the rudder responded too slowly. The fiberglass hull cut through the water on a direct collision course with Connor's head.

"Go astern," Brad ordered as Connor, unable to dive because of the life jacket, held up his arms to shield himself.

"Astern? What's astern?" cried Ling, her voice rising in pitch as the tender plowed toward Connor.

"*Reverse!*"

Connor could no longer see what was happening, but he heard a crunch of gears. When it came to piloting a boat, Ling was clearly more adept at speed than steering. The tender's engine roared, and the hull stopped within a fraction of Connor's head.

"Switch off the engine," shouted Brad, "before the propeller chops him into sushi."

He leaned over the bow rail and offered Connor a broad grin. "That was a close shave in more ways than one, wasn't it?"

By the time Ling appeared to help pull him aboard, the boat had drifted and Connor was once again beyond reach.

"You'll have to make another pass," said Brad.

Ling let out an exasperated sigh. She returned to the helm, started the engine and put it into reverse.

"No," said Brad. "If you go astern, you're in danger of butchering him."

"Why can't he just swim to us?" said Ling, her jaw set with frustration.

There was another crunch of gears. Brad raised his eyes to heaven, and Ling caught him in the act.

"Don't you dare say anything!" she muttered, hammering at the gears.

"Heaven forbid," replied Brad with his most guileless expression.

After three further attempts, Ling finally managed to

pull alongside Connor and safely haul him aboard single-handedly.

"Well, we got there in the end," said Brad, patting a seething Ling on the shoulder. "But I think we need a bit more practice at the man-overboard drill, don't you?"

He raised an eyebrow at Connor, who stood dripping wet on the deck.

"Are you willing to throw yourself over for another drill?"

"Sure," said Connor. "But only if Ling promises not to try to run me over again."

Ling narrowed her eyes at him. "Well, hotshot, maybe next time I'll leave you to the sharks!"

28

"Pirates always hold the advantage," explained Brad, leaning forward and resting his elbows on the table in the sky lounge. "As the hunter, they choose the time and place. And, of course, they know that a yacht like this is virtually defenseless."

"But what about NATO's counterpiracy operation?" asked Connor.

"Yeah," said Ling, through a mouthful of tuna salad. "They've got warships that can protect us."

Brad laughed, a deep booming sound as loud as a foghorn. "That naval task force is pretty much useless! It's not their fault, mind you. With just one small fleet in an ocean this size, it's like a single police car trying to patrol the whole of France. An impossible task. Therefore, at sea we're on our own. And we must be prepared to defend ourselves."

The week of intensive MARSEC training had flown by. The two of them were now proficient in reading radar, interpreting charts and using the yacht's comms equipment. Brad had also shown them how to tackle onboard fires, deploy a life raft and fire a flare gun, and what the emergency procedure was for abandoning ship. Now, over lunch, their mentor was briefing them on the ship's security plan in the event of a pirate attack.

"Our defense strategy is to Detect, Deter, Destroy," he said, thumping the tabletop to emphasize each stage. "As you already know, the key to thwarting pirates is to detect any possible attack *before* they can get alongside and board us. Once they know they've been spotted, they lose their element of surprise. From my experience, many will back off to wait for a less observant crew to sail past. So, to help us with that, we'll use the radar, binoculars, night-vision goggles and a twenty-four-hour watch shift."

"Will *we* be on lookout duty?" asked Connor.

Brad shook his head. "No, the crew might question your involvement. Between myself, the chief officer, Mr. Sterling's bodyguard and one of the deckhands, we'll cover that. But both of you still need to keep a sharp lookout. The more eyeballs, the better."

Brad took a sip of water and a bite of his sandwich.

"If we do run into pirates, our next step is to deter them," he continued, wiping his mouth with a napkin. "On a commercial ship, we would use razor wire, electrified fencing and water hoses. But I don't think Mr. Sterling would appreciate his fifty-million-dollar vacation yacht being turned into a battleship." Brad raised his eyebrows at his own suggestion. "So initially we'll have to rely on Captain Locke outrunning them and performing evasive maneuvers. Meanwhile, we'll try to attract attention with distress flares, searchlights, sirens and, of course, the radio."

Ling set aside her empty plate. "I hate to say this, but we've seen a video clip of a pirate attack. Their skiffs are pretty fast. And they have *rocket launchers*. I don't think a few flares and a bit of fancy sailing is going to dissuade them."

"Fair point," admitted Brad. "But most pirates prefer an easy target, so such a strategy can and often does work. Although you're right, some can be more determined. If that's the case, then we destroy them."

"So what weapons do we have?" Ling asked eagerly.

Brad offered an awkward smile. "That's a tricky issue. At sea, international law allows merchantmen to possess and use firearms for self-defense. But in most ports it's illegal to carry guns. So it's a bit of a catch-22 situation."

"Then what are we going to use?" asked Connor.

Brad raised his hands, palms up. "Pretty much anything goes. Although the *Orchid* is his pride and joy, I'll persuade the captain to ram the pirates. That'll be our most effective tactic. But it carries its own hazards, including damaging the screws and even holing the hull itself. So we'll also toss storage nets over the side to foul their outboard motors, and use the foam fire extinguishers to make the most accessible decks and stairways slippery. And, of course, fire flares directly at their skiffs."

He finished off his sandwich and put aside his plate.

"Once, I was on a ship where pirates managed to attach a grappling hook to the side. We threw a fridge full of Coca-Cola into their skiff!" Brad laughed at the recollection. "Their skiff took in so much water, they had to cut loose."

He waved a hand around the yacht.

"The prime objective is to keep the pirates from boarding the *Orchid*. Think of the hull and gunwales of this boat as castle walls. As long as they're not breached and the pirates don't reach the main deck, we're in a strong position."

Connor glanced down at the stern to where the tender garage was. The bay doors were open, and he could see the ship's engineer, a silver-bearded man by the name of Geoff, overseeing the delivery of a brand-new pair of Jet Skis. The tender garage was the lowest point of the yacht and appeared very vulnerable to Connor.

"What if the pirates do get aboard?" he asked.

"Then our last resort is the citadel," replied Brad.

Connor and Ling both gave him a perplexed look.

"Safe room," he clarified, pushing back his chair and beckoning them to follow him. They headed down the staircase to the main deck and through the galley before stopping beside a large bulkhead door.

"This leads to the crew's quarters and is our designated

citadel," explained Brad. He slapped the door with the palm of his hand. "This bulkhead can be double-locked from the inside. It's made of steel, so it's bulletproof. And down below we've got all we need to survive for several days—food, water, sanitation and, most importantly, communications equipment. If we're attacked, your first priority is to ensure the girls are inside the citadel. Then, God forbid, if the pirates do breach our defenses, along with the rest of the crew, we join them."

"But won't we be trapped?" said Ling.

Brad nodded emphatically. "That's the point. Trapped and safe. Once we're all inside the citadel, military forces can storm the ship with minimum risk to our lives. However, the citadel is effective only if *everyone* makes it inside."

"What a cheery conversation!" said a blond-haired young woman, emerging from the crew's quarters.

"Hi, Soph." Brad grinned, offering his most charming smile. "I was just explaining the emergency procedures to Mr. Sterling's guests."

Sophie, a young English stewardess from Southampton, gave Connor and Ling a sympathetic look. "Don't let him freak you out," she remarked. "Brad can be a little *anxious* before a sailing."

"Only because I want to keep everyone safe, including you, sweets."

Sophie arched an eyebrow at Brad, the corner of her

mouth curling into a coquettish smile, before strolling off down the corridor. Brad's eyes followed her a moment. Then he snapped back to the matter at hand.

"Well, that just about wraps up your training," he said, clapping his palms together and rubbing them. "All work and no play makes Jack a very dull boy. Take the afternoon off."

"Thanks," Connor replied, a little stunned by the sudden grant of leave.

"About time," muttered Ling under her breath.

Brad was halfway down the corridor before he turned back to them.

"Soph's right, though. I do get a bit edgy before a trip. But failure to prepare is preparing to fail. And our 'security lifeboat,' so to speak, needs to be watertight before sailing."

29

An elderly fisherman in a battered wooden skiff tossed a frayed net into the pale blue waters. Then he sat and waited. His cataract-clouded eyes drifted across the desolate coastline of chalk-streaked cliffs and bone-white sands until his blurred gaze reached the headland. It jutted out into the Indian Ocean like a skeletal finger. Behind his little fishing boat lay the rusting hulk of a long-abandoned cargo ship, hulled on a jagged rock. And beyond that on the horizon, like a mirage, were three more container ships. Not shipwrecked, he knew, but hijacked and held for ransom.

With slow, laborious effort, the fisherman pulled his net in, hand over hand, his ancient limbs protesting, until he was rewarded with . . . an empty net. He cursed the foreign trawlers who plundered all the fish from their waters without permission or conscience. Then he threw the net back into the sea and waited.

As the old man fished for nothing, six gleaming Toyota 4×4s raced across the desolate beach. Spitting sand from their tires, they were weaving dangerously between one another in a daredevil game of cat and mouse. One of the vehicles with a trailer attached threatened to roll over, but miraculously righted itself at the last second. Another cut through the shallows, sending up showers of spray. The 4×4s ground to a sudden halt beside a row of overturned skiffs on the shoreline.

Spearhead got out of the lead vehicle and started shouting orders to his men to unload. The band of pirates flung open their doors and began dragging out wooden boxes and large plastic fuel containers. Out of the back of the trailer, several pirates struggled with the enormous weight of a massive outboard motor, the first of four brand-new engines.

Stumbling across the burning sand, the skinny young pirate with buckteeth dropped one of the boxes and an assault rifle tumbled out, still in its protective packaging.

"Cool!" he said, kneeling down to retrieve the rifle. "Oracle got us new weapons."

"Move aside, Bucktooth, before you get hurt," said the pirate with sticking-out ears. Elbowing the boy out of the way, he picked up the rifle, slipped it from its protective wrapper and admired the well-oiled weapon. "AK-47. Chinese manufactured. Very reliable."

"Let me try it, Juggs," begged Bucktooth.

Juggs gave him a dismissive look. "These are for real men, not boys! Here, you can have this."

He passed Bucktooth an old revolver. The boy gazed at it in awe and grinned.

From another box, Juggs slammed a full magazine into the assault rifle and took casual aim at the nearby cliff face.

CLACK, CLACK, CLACK . . .

"*Wooooooo!*" he shouted above the roar of gunfire. The defenseless cliff spat shards of rock and dust as the barrage of bullets ripped into it.

"CEASE FIRE!" ordered Spearhead.

The earsplitting *crack* of the AK-47 echoed off the cliff, then faded.

"But there are *boxes* of them," protested Juggs, still grinning from ear to ear with the buzz of his newly acquired firepower.

"Then load the boxes onto the boats," snapped Spearhead, snatching away the weapon.

Juggs scowled but nonetheless bent down and heaved the ammo box across the sand.

The pirates worked slowly in the blistering sun, the harsh onshore wind offering no respite from the furnace-like heat. Gradually the skiffs filled with weapons, ammunition, diesel, navigation equipment, water and food supplies.

"And what have we got here?" muttered Big Mouth to

himself as he discovered a long wooden box in the back of the last 4×4. He jimmied off the lid and hefted out a brand-new rocket-propelled grenade launcher. Sifting through the paper-pulp packaging, he also uncovered several rockets. "I think I'm in love," he said, caressing one of the warheads.

With hands trembling from anticipation, he carefully loaded one of the rockets, shouldered the launcher and took aim at the rusted cargo ship in the bay.

"Look out for that old fisherman," warned Bucktooth as he eyed the formidable weapon with a mix of awe and fear.

"*He's* the one who should look out." With a crooked grin, Big Mouth depressed the trigger.

The rocket *whoosh*ed out of the launcher and scorched over the waves. Even at this distance, the pirates could see the old fisherman's face widen in terror. He dived into the waters just before the rocket passed over his little boat and struck the cargo ship behind him. There was a deep howl of twisting metal as a massive explosion ripped through the hull. The ship's fuel tanks ignited with the last of their diesel, and a ball of fire engulfed the entire bow. The little fishing skiff was caught in the expanding blast, disintegrating into a shower of flaming splinters.

"Did you see *that*?" whooped Big Mouth, dancing a jig on the beach. "These babies are tank-busters!"

The other pirates hollered and bent double with laughter as the fisherman's head bobbed back up amid the carnage of his fishing boat. He swam desperately for the shore, leaving his only means of scraping a living to float away in shattered pieces.

Spearhead stormed over to Big Mouth and shouted in his face, "What did you do THAT for?"

Wiping tears of laughter from his eyes, the pirate held up the RPG launcher. "Just checking its accuracy."

Spearhead clocked Big Mouth around the back of his head with an open palm, the slap almost as loud as the grenade explosion.

"*Ow!*" complained Big Mouth, shying away from their commander. The other pirates instantly stopped laughing.

"You'll buy that old man a new boat out of your ransom share," Spearhead ordered, "or I'll gut you like a tuna fish."

"Chill, Spearhead," replied Big Mouth, waving him away. "With the money we'll get, I'll buy that fishhead *two* boats."

30

"The white pickup truck you identified was a ringer," said Charley.

"A *ringer*?" repeated Connor, holding up his phone so that both he and Ling could see Charley's face on the screen. They huddled in a quiet area of the Seychelles International Airport while awaiting the arrival of Mr. Sterling's private jet.

"A stolen vehicle, its license plates swapped with a set from a totaled car," Charley explained. "There's no way we can trace the truck."

"What about the two muggers?" asked Ling.

"We had a bit more luck with them. Amir scoured security cameras from the local area and found a grainy shot of the two guys on Rollerblades. Using the Australian Criminal Intelligence Database, we've managed to identify the man with the tattoo as Todd Logan and his associate as Doug Carter."

Two mug shots, one of a grizzled white man, the other of a bald black man, filled the screen.

"They're both heavies-for-hire," Charley's voice continued in the background. "Linked to numerous criminal gangs, they have a list of convictions as long as their arms: robbery, drug dealing, extortion, arson and violent assault. You name it, they've probably done it. They were released only last month from prison. I guess they were desperate to earn a fast buck."

Connor exchanged a stunned look with Ling. Both realized how lucky they'd been to get away so lightly in the attack.

"So where are the men now?" asked Ling.

Charley's face reappeared on Connor's phone.

"The Sydney police haven't been able to track them down yet, but as soon as I hear anything, you'll be the first to know. In the meantime, I'll see what else I can dig up on them."

"Thanks," said Connor. "At least we've got decent ID shots of them now."

"All part of the service," said Amir, nudging into the frame beside Charley. "So how's the weather out there?"

"Oh, rainy, cold and miserable," sighed Ling, putting on her glummest expression.

"*Really?*" said Amir, his eyes widening in undisguised delight at the thought.

Connor couldn't help but laugh. "Of course not! It's eighty degrees and glorious sunshine."

Amir scowled. "Well, it's the same here," he said, "apart from the lack of sun and warmth. Anyway, I just wanted to check that my equipment is still functioning."

Connor waggled the sunglasses on his head. "All looking good."

Hearing his name being called, Connor glanced up to see Brad beckoning them to join him at the arrivals gate.

"Have to go," Connor explained to Amir. "Mr. Sterling's jet just landed."

"Oh, it's a hard life for some," said Amir in a gently mocking tone. "Give us a shout if you need anything *technical*."

"Stay sharp and stay safe," added Charley, before ending the video call.

Connor slipped the phone into the pocket of his polo shirt, the flotation cover making it too bulky for his shorts, then followed Ling across to Brad.

"Okay, guys, let's look professional," Brad said, breaking into a wide grin. "Now the hard work really begins."

Brad had already performed a security sweep of the airport terminal with their help and was satisfied that the location was secure. They watched through the window as the sleek Gulfstream jet taxied up to the private gate. After a minute or so, the aircraft's doors opened and a stairway unfolded. Mr. Sterling emerged followed by a slender blond woman with long tanned legs in a daringly short dress and high heels. With the poise of a professional model, she gracefully descended the steps to the runway.

"Pick your jaw up!" hissed Ling, glowering sideways at Connor.

Connor hadn't realized he was gawking. But he wasn't alone in his admiration. As Amanda Ryder sashayed into the terminal building, every man's head turned toward her. Rather than appear jealous, Mr. Sterling grinned from ear-to-ear, seeming to thrive on the attention his glamorous fiancée attracted.

As the couple approached, Mr. Sterling waved at his welcoming party. The tautness Connor had noticed in the man's features while in Sydney had softened, as if he'd left the burden of his work behind, but the media mogul's eyes still maintained their steely intensity.

"Good to see you both again," he said, nodding at Connor and Ling. "Brad, everything in order?"

"Yes, sir," replied Brad. "And may I welcome you to the Seychelles, Ms. Ryder."

"Why, thank you," she replied, her voice smooth as honey. She squeezed Mr. Sterling's arm affectionately. "But I hope I won't be using that name much longer."

In response, Mr. Sterling smiled and kissed her warmly on the cheek.

A respectful distance behind the couple stood Mr. Sterling's personal bodyguard, one of the few men in the terminal not to be admiring Ms. Ryder. Instead he focused on his new surroundings, offering a professional nod of courtesy to Brad in the process. Dressed in a short-sleeved shirt and chinos, he looked like any other tourist. And since he was wearing sunglasses, Connor couldn't read his expression when he also gave a barely perceptible acknowledgment to him and Ling. Recalling his briefing notes, Connor knew the man's name was Dan and that he'd been Mr. Sterling's close-protection officer ever since the last one was fired after Emily's kidnapping.

"And when will your daughters be joining us, sir?" Brad asked Mr. Sterling.

Just at that moment, the gate opened again and the girls entered, dressed in flowery summer tops and white shorts.

Brad gestured to Connor, who stepped forward to greet them. "Hi, Emily! Welcome to—"

"I'm *Chloe*," said the sister he was addressing. She flicked back a lock of straw-blond hair to reveal her ear. "I have a mole on my right earlobe; Emily doesn't, if that helps."

"Sorry," said Connor, unable to believe he'd made such a faux pas.

"So how was your flight?" asked Ling, swiftly moving on from Connor's mistake as Mr. Sterling informed Brad of his plans for the vacation.

"Fine, although I never can sleep on planes," replied Emily. She offered them both an awkward smile. "Look, I want to apologize for my behavior the first time we met."

"Nothing to apologize for," said Connor diplomatically.

"No, I was rude and ill-mannered." She glanced in the direction of her father, who was being escorted by Brad toward the exit. Still she lowered her voice. "I was angry at my father, not you. But you proved your worth in Sydney. So I hope . . . we can make a fresh start."

"Of course," said Connor, shaking the hand she offered. "Forget it ever happened."

"Thanks." Emily tried unsuccessfully to stifle a yawn. "Sorry, long trip."

"Shall we make a move to the yacht, then?" he suggested. "You can rest and freshen up."

Emily smiled and nodded.

Chloe was already skipping off toward the exit. "Absolutely. We're missing out on valuable sunbathing time."

Ling called after her Principal. "You've forgotten your bag," she said, pointing to a small wheeled carry-on case.

Chloe barely glanced over her shoulder. "No, I think *you've* forgotten my bag."

Ling frowned and shot Connor a questioning look. Their instructor Jody had taught them that a bodyguard always needed to keep their hands free so they could react quickly to a sudden threat. Carrying the bags or belongings of a Principal immediately limited a bodyguard's response time.

Connor shrugged in response. Ling was left with little other choice than to do as she was told. By now Chloe was almost at the exit and would soon be out of sight. *That* was an even more risky situation for a bodyguard. Huffing to herself, Ling snatched the bag's handle and hurried after her Principal.

31

"I wouldn't recommend sunbathing under that tree," said Connor as Chloe and Emily laid their towels on the pristine beach.

"Why not?" said Emily, the corner of her lips curling up into a tease. "Worried about dropbears?"

"Not this time," Connor replied with a glance up into the canopy. "Coconuts."

As if to prove his point, a large brown husk fell from a nearby palm and plopped heavily into the sand. Brad had warned Connor about the danger, recounting a story of an old rock star who'd had his skull cracked open by one.

Emily and Chloe quickly retrieved their towels.

"So where *do* you suggest?" asked Chloe.

"Try this one," said Ling, patting the trunk of a tall tree with thick waxy-green leaves. "It's a takamaka—no danger of falling nuts here."

Upon the instruction of Mr. Sterling, Captain Locke had

sailed the *Orchid* around the southern tip of Mahé Island to Anse Takamaka, a secluded beach named after the abundance of the tree species. The idyllic horseshoe bay was like a scene straight out of *Robinson Crusoe*, pure white sand fringed with palms and crystal-blue waves rippling along the shoreline.

Chloe repositioned her towel, lay down and stretched herself out in the sun. "Now, this is the life," she said, taking out a glossy magazine, sunscreen, headphones and her smartphone from her beach bag.

Joining her sister, Emily had an equal array of light entertainment, but ignored it in favor of watching the white-tailed birds and multicolored butterflies flitting among the lush vegetation surrounding them. The beach was utterly unspoiled by human habitation. Mr. Sterling and Ms. Ryder were relaxing on beach chairs brought over on the tender. Sophie and another stewardess were serving them drinks and ensuring their every need was met. The girls had decided they wanted to be farther down the beach, away from the doting couple, and Mr. Sterling hadn't objected as long as Connor and Ling accompanied them.

Connor and Ling put down their go-bags and prepared for a day of sunbathing. As Ling got out her towel, she gave Connor a sly grin and whispered, "This is going to be a breeze if all we have to worry about are coconuts!"

Looking up and down the deserted beach, Connor couldn't help but agree. There was no one who could hassle the girls, and there were no apparent threats: just glorious sun, sand and sea. The recipe for a perfect vacation.

Connor riffled through his go-bag for sunscreen and the paperback book he'd bought at the airport, then sat down and did another visual sweep of the area. The coast was utterly clear. No other boats, aside from the *Orchid* anchored beyond the bay.

"You can take first watch," said Ling, lying back on her towel and closing her eyes.

But no sooner had Ling gotten comfortable than Chloe said, "Ling, get me a drink."

Ling sat back up, a flicker of irritation passing across her face before asking, "What would you like?"

Chloe waved a hand in the direction of the tender. "Chef should have packed a pitcher of fresh lemonade."

"Ooh, that sounds good," said Emily. "Can I have one too?"

"Of course," said Ling, getting to her feet. "I'll bring the whole pitcher." She strode over to where Sophie was talking with Brad and Dan near the moored tender.

. While Ling was busy collecting the drinks, Emily turned to Connor. "Would you mind blowing up my floating mattress for me, please? I'd like to go lounge in the water."

"Sure," said Connor, delving into his go-bag and retrieving

the inflatable silver mattress he'd been given earlier. Putting the valve to his lips, he began the slow process of blowing it up.

Ling returned with a tray of four iced lemonades and the pitcher. Chloe downed hers in one gulp, asked for another, then plugged in her earphones and lay facedown on her towel. Once Emily got her drink, Ling offered a glass to Connor, who was still puffing away.

"Thanks," he gasped, taking a large gulp of lemonade, its ice-cold zest refreshing him. After a dozen more lungfuls of air, the mattress was fully inflated.

"Here you go," said Connor.

"Great," said Emily, taking the inflatable mattress and trotting down to the shoreline.

While Emily paddled in the shallows and her sister lay sprawled in the sun, Connor and Ling were left to their own devices. With nothing to do, Ling stretched out on her towel and sunbathed too. Seeing Emily happily floating on the water, Connor picked up his book and began to read.

After a while, Brad strolled over. "I'm just taking Mr. Sterling and Ms. Ryder back to the boat. I'll return to collect the girls for lunch. All good here?"

Connor nodded. Chloe was laid out, eyes closed and humming to a song on her headphones, while Emily still lay on her mattress, bobbing gently on the waves.

"Well, don't work too hard!" warned Brad with a playful wink.

Connor heard the tender depart, then settled back into his book.

He'd read only a couple of chapters when Ling sat up and nudged him.

"Do you think Emily's all right?"

Connor looked up. Emily was flat out on her mattress, almost a hundred feet from the shore. Last time he'd looked, she had been only some thirty feet away.

Putting aside his book, Connor jogged down to the waterline. "Emily," he called.

But she didn't respond. By the looks of it, she'd fallen asleep. With a growing sense of panic, Connor realized her inflatable mattress was caught in a current and she was drifting fast out to sea.

32

"EMILY!" Connor shouted again. But she still didn't wake up. Either she was too far out to hear him or she *couldn't* wake up. With the six-hour time difference between the Seychelles and Sydney and the drowsy side effects of her medication, her body clock was probably out of sync.

He looked to the *Orchid* at the opposite end of the bay. The tender was tethered to its stern, and he couldn't see anyone on deck. And there were, of course, no lifeguards on this deserted beach. In the few seconds Connor had taken to search for help, Emily had drifted even farther out. If he didn't take immediate action, she'd soon be lost in open water.

"I'm going to bring her back," Connor told Ling, ripping off his T-shirt and running into the sea. "Contact Brad."

As soon as he was deep enough, he dived beneath the waves and swam hard. Surfacing, he powered through the water, glad now for all of Charley's training.

But swimming in the sea was totally different from being in an indoor pool. Although the bay was relatively calm, the gentle swell still blocked his line of sight. Emily and her silver inflatable mattress continually bobbed in and out of view, and he had to keep stopping to ensure he was still heading in the right direction.

Emily was now more than 250 feet out, almost beyond the tip of the headland. Connor dug deep with every ounce of strength he possessed. His legs kicking, his arms pumping, he swam not for his life, but for hers.

Then all of a sudden he was alongside her.

"Emily!" he gasped, clutching the mattress's handle.

But she was still dead to the world, a blissful smile on her face.

Deciding that waking her suddenly at this point could risk her drowning, Connor turned the mattress around and kicked for the shore. After a minute or so, he looked up. The beach seemed no closer.

He put his head down and kicked furiously, driving the inflatable mattress ahead of him.

Connor looked up again. They were still beyond the headland. He realized he wasn't getting anywhere. He was fighting *against* the current.

Despair crept into his mind. There was no way he could beat the pull of the ocean. His heart was already pounding like a drum, and he could feel his muscles burning from the effort made just to reach Emily.

Where is Brad and the tender?

He would never rescue Emily at this rate. Then he remembered Charley reminiscing about one of her surfing trips where she'd been caught in a riptide. These currents, she'd explained, were rarely more than a hundred feet wide, and surfers often used them as an expressway into the ocean to catch waves. The way to escape a riptide was to simply swim parallel to the shore and, once clear, diagonally back to the beach.

Redirecting their path, Connor swam toward the headland. Then, as soon as he judged he was clear of the rip, he took a diagonal course to where Ling stood waving to him.

With a glance over at the headland, Connor saw he was at last making progress. But the going was still tough. His lungs burned for air, and to make matters worse, in his growing exhaustion he started to lose his rhythm. His limbs grew heavy as lead, and he imagined himself sinking to the seabed like a stone.

In the distance he could hear the roar of the motorboat's engines.

Then, all of a sudden, his foot struck sand, and he glanced up in surprise.

"Are you okay?" asked Ling, pulling the inflatable mattress and Emily onto the foreshore. Farther up the beach, Chloe was still stretched out on her towel, headphones on, oblivious to the near tragedy. Brad was just arriving in the tender.

Connor dragged himself out of the shallows and collapsed on the warm sand. "Barely," he wheezed as a wave of white water rushed up the beach, engulfing the mattress and waking Emily with a start.

"Oh . . . I must have dozed off," she said, sitting up and brushing her wet hair from her face. Seeing Connor sprawled in the sand like a beached fish, gasping for breath, she remarked, "Did you go for a swim?"

Connor opened his mouth to reply but was too exhausted for words and just let his head flop back down.

"You need to relax more," Emily said, laughing. "This is a vacation, you know."

33

Oracle regarded his loose band of pirates through the tinted passenger window of his Land Cruiser. The men lolled in the meager shade of a ramshackle fisherman's hut, bored and listless in the unrelenting heat. Only the young pirate Bucktooth crouched in the full glare of the sun, forced to remain on guard by the skiffs. An unnecessary duty, imposed by the other pirates as a cruel prank, since no villager or fisherman would dare approach Oracle's gang or their boats. But the boy appeared happy enough with his revolver to carry out the duty.

Picking up the slim cell phone from the seat beside him, Oracle pressed the speed-dial number. After several distant rings, he heard a click and his investor answered. "Yes?"

"My men are ready," informed Oracle.

There was a crackle on the line, the signal poor at the base of the cliff, but he could just make out his investor's response. "Have . . . supplies . . . arrived?"

"Yes," replied Oracle. "And Mr. Wi-Fi has tracked down the target to its current location in Victoria Harbor. We'll be there by—"

"Your information is out of date . . . The yacht is now at Anse Takamaka . . . Tomorrow . . . sail to Bel Ombre . . . after that to Praslin Island."

Oracle's brow furrowed slightly. "How do *you* know the yacht's itinerary?"

As Oracle listened to the reply, his upper lip curled into an astonished smirk. "That is quite something . . . Yes, I'll keep you fully informed of our progress."

Snapping shut the phone, Oracle lowered his passenger window. A rush of hot dry air invaded the vehicle's cool interior as Spearhead's sweating face appeared.

"Get the men boarded," instructed Oracle.

"Yes, boss. Are we still headed for the Seychelles?"

Oracle nodded. "At this moment, yes, but Mr. Wi-Fi will send you updates via the satellite link."

Spearhead gave a dismissive snort and waved his hand at a buzzing fly. "That's all well and good, but his hacked coordinates are always out by a few hours because of the security delay. Sometimes the ship is over the horizon by the time we get there."

Oracle offered a smug grin. "Not this time. The investor is able to supply the *real-time* location of the *Orchid*."

Spearhead's eyes widened in his head, and he grunted an

incredulous laugh. "Then this is gonna be like shooting fish in a barrel."

"Let the game begin," Oracle commanded, winding up his window and barring the all-pervading heat.

As the Land Cruiser sped away across the baking sand, Spearhead barked orders at his men. Idle from chewing khat all morning, the pirates rose to their feet and trudged down the beach to their boats. They threw nets over their weapons and supplies to make it look as though they were legitimate fishermen. Pushing the boats from the shoreline, the pirates clambered aboard and started their engines. The powerful outboard motors roared, churning up a flurry of white water as the small armada of pirate skiffs surged out of the bay.

34

"Pirates!" shouted Chloe. "Pirates ahoy!"

"Where?" said Connor, looking to the horizon, his pulse immediately racing. The glassy sea was a mirror to the blue sky, the line between heaven and earth lost in the distant haze. Aside from the *Orchid*, there were five other yachts anchored around the picturesque bay in Bel Ombre on the island's northwest coast. Beyond those, a few fishing boats bobbed out at sea. But Connor couldn't see any skiffs armed with RPGs powering toward them.

"Shiver me timbers, Connor, I was only joking!" said Chloe, giggling at his overreaction. "But you never know, we might find some pirate treasure in here."

She ducked inside a large dark hole in the cliff face. Taking a break from yesterday's sunbathing, the four of them were exploring the headland of the bay. Clambering over granite boulders and through warm barnacled rock pools, they'd managed to reach the outermost tip.

"Hold up," cried Ling, who'd also been fooled by Chloe's pirate prank. "It could be dangerous in there."

"You two *really* need to lighten up," said Chloe, her reply echoing out of the cave mouth.

Ling disappeared after her Principal, but Emily hesitated at the entrance, eyeing the dark opening with mistrust.

"Are you all right with this?" asked Connor.

"Why shouldn't I be?" she replied, but a nervous swallow betrayed her true feelings.

Connor tried to make eye contact. "You don't have to go in—"

"Come on, Emily!" Chloe called, her voice now eerily distant. "You have to see this."

Taking a deep breath, Emily plunged into the darkness.

Connor kept close on her heels. After the inflatable mattress incident the previous day, he wasn't allowing himself to become complacent on the assignment again. He had to be ready for anything, danger lying in the most innocent of activities.

The hole narrowed to a passageway that burrowed deep into the headland. At first there was just blackness, but as Connor's eyes adjusted to the lack of light, he could make out the multitude of mollusks clinging to the hard, moist rock. After a dozen or so paces, the passageway opened out into a large cavern, a crack in the overhead rock letting in a feeble shaft of sunlight. The air within was as cool and damp as a tomb, and he felt his skin goose bump at the sudden drop in temperature.

"Over here," said Chloe, beckoning them to the far wall. Ling stood beside her, both their faces in shadow, as they inspected the faintly gleaming surface.

Connor followed Emily across the cavern, their feet crunching through the coarse sand and broken shells on the uneven floor.

"Check these out," said Chloe excitedly, pointing to some symbols on the wall. Into the rock had been carved a dog, a snake, two joined hearts, a keyhole, a staring eye, a figure of a woman's body and the head of a man.

"Creepy," said Ling.

The boom of a crashing wave rebounded and amplified inside the cavern space. Connor glanced across at Emily, who'd become strangely quiet and withdrawn. In the feeble light, he could see that she was trembling and that a sheen of sweat had broken out on her forehead.

"Emily?" asked Connor. But she didn't reply.

Chloe ran her finger over the staring eye. "I read in a guidebook that some pirate supposedly buried his treasure on this island. On his death at the gallows, he left a cryptic map to its location," she explained. "This must be one of the clues . . ."

Emily now appeared to be struggling for breath.

"I think it's time to make a move," Connor suggested,

taking Emily by the arm and guiding her back toward the tunnel.

"In a minute," said Chloe, too engrossed in studying the symbols to notice her sister's distress. "Maybe we can figure out what this says . . ."

Emily let out a doglike whimper.

Chloe turned to her sister. "Are you all right, Em?"

Her eyes had gone white with fear, and she stared in blind panic at the cave entrance. A huge shadow slipped along the mollusk-encrusted wall, threatening in both its size and silence.

"I'll do what you say . . ." she whispered in a breath almost too quiet to hear. "I'll do what you say . . . I'll do what you say . . ."

Connor drew Emily closer as she repeated the words like a mantra. A muscle-bound man now blocked their only exit.

"Hope I didn't scare you," said Brad. "But the tide's coming in, and these caves are prone to flooding."

35

"Don't forget to put the kill cord around your wrist," reminded Ling as she zipped up her life jacket.

"I know," snapped Chloe, straddling the Jet Ski. "I have ridden these things before."

"Sorry—just going through the safety checks," replied Ling in a defensive tone as she clambered aboard the other one. "Don't want it running away from you."

Chloe, her hair tied back in a ponytail, looked over her shoulder at her sister. "Sure you don't want to come with us?"

"Maybe later," replied Emily with a strained smile.

"How about you, Connor?" asked Chloe. "You can ride with me if you want."

Connor eyed the sleek Jet Ski. He was itching to try it, but he couldn't leave his Principal. "I'd love to, but I'll stick with Emily on the beach."

"Your loss," she sighed, and she pressed the Jet Ski's ignition.

Over the thrum of the engine, they heard Amanda shout out, "Have fun!"

She waved cheerily to them, looking glamorous as ever in a straw sunhat, white midriff blouse and sarong. Mr. Sterling, his arm around her waist, raised a hand as the two of them headed to a local beach bar, where Dan had reserved a private table.

"Off go the lovebirds again," Chloe muttered without bothering to wave back. Twisting the throttle, she sped off across the water. As Ling depressed her Jet Ski's starter, there was a slight splutter from the exhaust, and then she raced off after her Principal.

After watching Chloe and Ling zip back and forth a couple of times, Connor suggested a stroll along the beach.

"Are you feeling any better now?" he asked Emily.

She glanced sideways at him. "You noticed, then."

Connor nodded. "We're briefed on things like that," he said, not wishing to worry her about how obvious the panic attack had been.

Emily let out a heavy sigh. "Yeah, I suppose you are. Well, after what happened last year, I get very anxious in such places. My mind becomes foggy and I sort of . . . blank out."

"Then why did you go in?"

Emily dug a toe into the sand. "To try to beat my fear."

Connor smiled, his respect for her growing at such

strength of character. "I can relate to that. I've been in a similar situation."

Emily looked up in shock. "Really? When?"

"Just this year," Connor admitted. "I can't tell you any details, but I was held captive for a number of days."

Emily studied his face, concern now etching her brow. "I had no idea. How are you coping?"

Connor shrugged. "Okay, I suppose. I didn't really think about it much at the time. I was concentrating on protecting my Principal."

Emily nodded. "I suppose that must have helped. To have someone else to focus on, I mean." She looked off toward the horizon, a haunted look in her eyes. "I was completely alone."

In the background, the Jet Skis buzzed like hornets above the gentle wash of the waves.

"That must have been hard for you," said Connor.

"You don't know the half of it," she said, her voice wavering with emotion. "The isolation was torture. I've been beside my sister all my life. I was desperate for her company, for a friend, *anyone* . . ." She turned to look at him as if to say more, but the noise from the Jet Ski engines suddenly reached a whirring pitch. Then there was a huge *BANG*.

Connor spun around to see Ling tumbling head over heels through the air, her Jet Ski in flames. He was already running down the beach and through the waves by the time she splashed into the sea. Chloe zoomed over, picking up Connor halfway as he swam to Ling's rescue.

Ling floated limp in the emerald-green waters. Her Jet Ski was melting into a blob of plastic and black smoke. Connor leaped from the back of Chloe's craft and grabbed Ling by her life jacket.

"Ling, speak to me!"

Her eyes flickered, and she gradually focused on Connor's face. "Wow . . . that was *wild*."

"Are you hurt?" asked Connor.

Ling gazed drowsily down at herself, then at the surrounding water. "There's . . . no blood . . . so I don't think so."

"What happened?" demanded Connor as he helped her onto Chloe's Jet Ski.

"The throttle got stuck . . . then it just *exploded*."

36

"Connor, I need your protection!"

Connor immediately looked over to where Chloe was laid out on the *Orchid*'s sundeck. In a canary-yellow bikini and sunglasses, she was wagging a bottle of suntan lotion at him. Connor rose from his chair, then noticed Ling, who was filling out an accident report for Brad, glance up and roll her eyes. Connor now hesitated, wondering if applying sunscreen would cross the line of appropriate behavior with a Principal.

"Please?" insisted Chloe, lowering her sunglasses, her expression all sweet innocence. "I can't reach my back."

Ling tutted quietly to herself as Connor went over. He replied with a shrug as if to say, *What else can I do?* It wasn't as if the request was unusual, considering the circumstances.

"Thanks," said Chloe, settling facedown on the padded sun bed attached to the hot tub.

As Connor dutifully rubbed the lotion on Chloe's back,

Ling continued with the accident report. She'd been extremely fortunate to get away with only a few scrapes and bruises, the worst injury being a minor burn on the inside of her left thigh. Not only had the water cushioned her fall and extinguished any flames, but her fire-retardant T-shirt and shorts had protected her from the worst of the explosion.

The remains of the offending Jet Ski were now with the Seychelles coast guard, pending an investigation into the cause of the accident. Profusely apologetic to Ling, Geoff, the ship's engineer, was at a loss about how it could have happened in the first place, since the Jet Skis were brand-new. Ling herself was surprisingly relaxed about the whole affair, although she gladly accepted Brad's proposal of an afternoon off to fully recover.

Emily emerged from the staircase, raised an eyebrow at her sister having suntan lotion applied by Connor, then turned to Ling. "How are you feeling, Ling?"

"Fine, thank you," she replied. "The burn cream is working great."

Emily strolled over to the handrail. With her back to Connor and her sister, she admired the view as the *Orchid* eased away from Bel Ombre for their next destination. Holding up her phone, she took a photo of the picture-perfect bay.

As Emily tapped away on the screen, Ling glanced over in curiosity. "Did you just post that photo online?"

Emily looked over. "Sorry, what was that?"

"I asked if you'd posted that on Instagram, or Facebook, or some other site."

Emily nodded with a smile. "The view's too good not to share."

"Next time, don't."

"Why on earth can't she?" said Chloe, raising herself onto her elbows and glaring at Ling. "I did exactly the same back on the beach."

Ling put down her pen. "The problem is your phone automatically adds your location to the photos, letting people know where you are and when."

Chloe looked at Ling as if she were dumb. "Duh! That's the whole point."

"It's a security breach," insisted Ling, holding Chloe's glare.

Chloe groaned. "Jeez, you're being paranoid. Your accident must have spooked you. Besides, I want my friends to know where I am. So, don't tell us what to do and what not to do."

Feeling the tension rise, Connor stepped in to back Ling up. "It's not your friends we're worried about," he explained gently. "It's *anyone else* who may be following your profile."

"Like who?"

"Those muggers back in Sydney."

"Oh, please. We're thousands of miles from there."

"Okay, I'll be more careful in the future," Emily cut in. She offered Ling an appeasing smile. "But I really can't imagine anyone would be interested in our vacation pictures."

37

The first stars pinpricked the sky as the horizon purpled with the coming of night. In the deepening twilight, the cluster of pirate skiffs powered over the waves, their outboards purring steadily. Spearhead crouched in the bow of the lead boat, his eyes adjusting to the growing darkness. His body had long since become accustomed to the constant to-and-fro of the ocean's swell, and he simply conserved his energy for the forthcoming attack.

As promised, Mr. Wi-Fi had forwarded the updated coordinates—the *Orchid* was now en route to Praslin Island. Spearhead honestly believed that this would be the easiest hijacking in all his four short years as a pirate. If the bounty was as large as Oracle had hinted at, then he could retire for the rest of his life, bathed in riches and beautiful women. But, despite the lure of such a lifestyle, he knew in his heart of hearts that he could never give up the pirate life. The urgent thrill of the chase was like a drug to him, almost as addictive as the power he wielded over a hijacked ship and its pathetic crew.

"Hey!" called Big Mouth from an adjacent skiff.

Spearhead directed his gaze southeast to where Big Mouth was pointing. On the distant horizon, like a gleaming jewel, was the outline of a white luxury yacht. Spearhead considered the vessel for a few moments, then signaled to the other skiffs, moving his hand in a serpent-like fashion and pointing to the target. Then he signed to Big Mouth's boat to circle around and approach from the opposite direction.

They were still over three miles away, so at this stage of the attack, stealth was the preferred strategy. With his boat leading the way, the skiffs zigzagged across the waves, gradually closing in on their target from the stern to avoid the yacht's radar.

The darkness of night descended, and only the silvery gleam of a half-moon lit their approach. But the yacht's owners were considerate enough to leave on their navigation lights. Like moths to a lamp, the pirates converged on the unsuspecting vessel.

As the skiffs came within ambush distance, the buzz of adrenaline rushed through Spearhead's veins. The other pirates in his boat had fallen silent, equally edgy yet exhilarated at the imminent attack.

At less than a quarter of a mile out, someone on the yacht's deck spotted Big Mouth's boat. There was a cry of alarm, and a searchlight was pointed in its direction. The VHF radio in Spearhead's skiff burst into life as the captain of the yacht demanded that the approaching boat identify itself. Big Mouth responded with a hail of gunfire across the yacht's bow.

But that was all good. Big Mouth was the distraction.

As the yacht's engines burst into life and tried to make an escape, Spearhead shouted to his pilot, "GO! GO! GO!"

The mighty outboards roared, and the skiff's bow rose high in the air as it plowed through the waves. The other skiffs joined in the pursuit, swarming toward the defenseless yacht. In less than a minute, the target vessel was surrounded on all sides.

However, the yacht's crew wasn't going to surrender without a fight. A flare was shot across the bow of one of the skiffs, and the yacht began to fishtail erratically in an attempt to ram any approaching pirates and make boarding impossible.

Despite the danger, Spearhead's pilot brought their skiff alongside the yacht's stern, bumping hard against the hull. Spearhead flung a grappling hook over the rail. It held fast, but the yacht suddenly veered away and the gap between the boats became treacherously wide. This was how Spearhead had earned his nickname: fearless, ruthless and admittedly a little crazy, he *spearheaded* every assault. He was the one who took the major risk of boarding first. And the rewards were greater for it.

With his AK-47 slung across his back and his hands gripping the rope, Spearhead leaped for the yacht's stern. He didn't make it, and his bare feet trailed in the water as he was dragged along by the speeding yacht. He tried to gain purchase on the hull, but the fiberglass was slick and icy smooth. Sea spray blinded him, and his body was battered against the hull as the yacht suddenly changed direction. Gritting his teeth, Spearhead clung on to the rope. Then, with a Herculean effort, he hauled himself up, hand over hand, to the lower-deck level.

Vaulting the safety rail, he unslung his AK-47 and prepared to take the yacht by force. A man carrying a flare suddenly appeared from behind a bulkhead. Shocked by the pirate's unexpected appearance on deck, he started to raise his hands. Spearhead slammed the butt of his rifle into the man's jaw. The sailor dropped to the ground, no longer capable of being a threat.

With the single-mindedness of a leopard stalking its prey, Spearhead prowled the main deck, searching the unfamiliar ship for the way to the bridge.

Another sailor emerged, and Spearhead leveled his AK-47 at him.

"Bridge?" he demanded.

The man cowered back into his cabin, pointing to a set of steps. Spearhead swiftly bounded up them and kicked open a wooden door. On the other side, the captain was shouting into the radio. "Mayday, Mayday, Mayday! This is motor yacht *Sunriser—*"

"STOP!" snarled Spearhead, planting the barrel of his AK-47 against the captain's temple.

His eyes wide with panic, the captain let the receiver drop to the floor. "Please . . . don't kill me."

Spearhead's maniacal grin flashed in the darkness. "I won't. As long as you do *exactly* as I say."

38

"Sure you don't want to join us?" asked Emily.

Chloe wrinkled her nose at her sister. "Why would I want to walk around a hot, wet forest?"

Emily shrugged. "For something different to do. Vallée de Mai is a World Heritage Site."

"No, thanks. I'm perfectly fine." Sipping from a freshly opened coconut, Chloe settled back on her beach chair beside the palm-thatched bar on Anse Volbert. She closed her eyes and sighed contentedly.

The exquisite beach, an unbroken line of silky white sand fringed by lush green takamaka trees, stretched the entire length of the bay. At anchor in its crystal-clear waters, the *Orchid* held court over the other luxury sailing yachts and catamarans moored off Praslin Island. Brad had just returned the tender to the yacht, having dropped off Mr. Sterling and his fiancée at an exclusive golf and spa resort on the island's northwestern tip. This meant the girls had the whole day to themselves—but Emily was impatient for a change of scenery.

"Don't get lost," said Ling, waving Connor off and grinning as she too made herself comfortable on a beach chair.

Taking a little yellow taxi, Connor and Emily were delivered five minutes later outside the entrance to Vallée de Mai. A small group of tourists were filing past a rustic wooden ticket office that marked the start of the forest trail. Connor paid the entrance fee, and he and Emily took the sandy path into the eco-reserve. A tangle of green fronds enveloped them, and they were soon immersed in an Eden-like setting.

"Vallée de Mai is the only place on earth where you can see the rare coco-de-mer palms," explained Emily, reading from the pamphlet she'd been given. "The palms produce the largest seed in the plant kingdom."

"No kidding," said Connor. "Look at the size of them!"

On a wooden bench beside the trail, three massive heart-shaped nuts had been laid out. Emily tried to pick one up and almost toppled over with the weight. Laughing, Connor tried to lift it. It was as big as his upper torso and heavier than a medicine ball, and even he struggled with the enormous seed.

"Supposedly they have aphrodisiac properties," said Emily, referring to the pamphlet.

"Aphro-what?"

"You know . . ." said Emily, a slight flush to her cheeks, "*romantic* effects."

"Really?" said Connor, quickly putting down the two-lobed nut.

Emily laughed and said, "Only when eaten."

Connor stared at the massive seed. "What? All of it?"

They exchanged amused glances, then sniggered to each other. As a middle-aged couple strolled up behind them, they stifled their laughs and continued down the path. They trekked more deeply into the emerald-tinged undergrowth, and the atmosphere became almost eerie, the dappled sunlight occasionally disappearing altogether beneath the monstrous corrugated leaves of the coco-de-mer trees. Like giant umbrellas, the fan palms soared a hundred feet up to a shadowy canopy where unseen creatures flitted from branch to branch.

"This place is like a real-life Jurassic Park," breathed Connor, gazing around at the primeval forest.

The call of bulbul birds and the whistling of black parrots sounded among the trees. The air was heavy with the odor of decaying vegetation and the sweet scent of flowering orchids. At any moment, Connor expected a pack of velociraptors to burst from the undergrowth and surround them.

As they wound their way along the path, Emily turned to him, her eyes downcast. "You know . . . I've not met anyone quite like you before," she admitted.

Connor glanced sideways at her, wondering where this conversation was going.

"I mean," she quickly added, "who could understand my *experience*."

Connor smiled gently. "Well, I've only got a notion of what you went through. I was a hostage for a few days. You were held for months."

"Yeah, and it felt like years," she said, running her fingers through the fronds of a fern. "But it *never* had to be that way."

"What do you mean?"

Emily looked up at the canopy where a bright green frog clung motionless to a palm leaf. "My father wouldn't pay the ransom. He abandoned me."

Connor tried to hide the shock on his face. "I'm sure he . . . he was advised to get proof of life before paying anything," he said, fumbling for a logical reason.

Emily shook her head gravely. "My father has always been a ruthless businessman. That's why he's so successful. The kidnappers were originally asking for five million dollars. At first he plain refused. Then he bargained them down. And down."

No wonder Mr. Sterling's so rich, thought Connor, *if he can play hardball with his daughter's life at stake.*

"But isn't that just part of the normal negotiation process?"

"I suppose so, but he reduced them to five *hundred thousand* dollars in the end." Emily looked Connor in the face, her eyes shining with tears. "He makes more than that in a week! Just goes to show how much my father values me."

Connor shifted awkwardly on the balls of his feet, uncertain what to say. He watched as another party of tourists made its way through the forest toward them. "Look, I'm not really in a position to judge. But your father has hired me and Ling to protect you and your sister. Surely that proves he cares for you."

Emily's gaze returned to the tree frog, which still hadn't moved. "For my sister, at least," she mumbled, then walked on.

Connor remained by her side as she continued to talk. "Chloe and I may look the same. But in truth we're yin and yang. I have no interest in business, media or socializing. That's why Chloe's always been the favorite. My father expects her to succeed him in managing his empire."

"But your sister doesn't seem too happy with him at the moment."

"That's because of *Amanda*," said Emily, her tone hardening. "We're supposed to be on vacation as a family, yet we've barely seen our father."

Out of nowhere the hairs on Connor's neck rose. He had the distinct feeling of being watched. His alert level went up a notch from Code Yellow to Code Orange. While pretending to admire the forest, he swept his gaze over the faces of the tourists behind them.

"I suppose it's understandable, in a way," Connor said,

spotting a black man in wraparound sunglasses and a blue baseball hat. The tourist was studying his pamphlet and purposefully not looking in their direction. "They seem very much in love."

"That's the problem. And it's not helped by the fact that Amanda is so"—Emily appeared to struggle for the right word—"self-centered. She only shows interest in us when our father's around. It seems like an act. Chloe's feeling pushed out by him, and she's really not used to that."

Sliding his phone from his pocket, Connor accessed the mug shot of the criminal Doug Carter on his screen. He tried to match the faces, but it was difficult since the tourist's features were mostly hidden by his hat and sunglasses. Still, Connor's sixth sense was twitching.

"I can see how Amanda's presence could cause problems," Connor replied, his attention now half on the man behind them. "Tell you what, shall we go back to the beach? I spotted a cool-looking ice-cream hut. They have mango and coconut flavors."

"Do they have coco-de-mer flavor too?"

Connor glanced at Emily, surprised, then realized she was attempting to make a joke. "Well, let's find out," he said, smiling.

Following the circular trail around to the entrance, Connor subtly checked behind them. The suspect man had broken away from the rest of the tourists and was keeping pace with them. Connor went to Code Red. *High alert.* Exiting the nature reserve as fast as he could, Connor hurried Emily over to the waiting taxi.

"You must be desperate for ice cream," she said, laughing as he opened the door for her and clambered in after her. Connor was now glad he'd been wise enough to pay the driver extra to wait for them. As the taxi pulled away, he glanced through the rear windshield. The man with wraparound sunglasses had disappeared.

"Are you all right?" asked Emily.

"Yeah, just thought I saw someone I knew," Connor replied, allowing his alert level to return to Code Yellow, "but I was wrong."

When they returned to the beach, Chloe and Ling were surrounded by a group of boys. Ling stood chatting with one of them, keeping a cautious eye on the scene. Chloe was fully reclined, teasing a lock of hair with a finger while laughing with two boys perched on the end of her beach chair. She looked over and waved excitedly as Connor and Emily approached.

"We've been invited to a beach party!"

39

"How convinced are you it was him?" asked Ling, digging her toes into the soft warm sand.

She and Connor sat a little distance from the bonfire, the wood crackling and sending sparks like fireflies into the night sky. Bathed in the flickering glow of the flames, they kept a careful watch on Chloe and Emily dancing and chatting with the other guests at the beach party. Initially Mr. Sterling hadn't been at all comfortable with the idea of his daughters attending. But Amanda had convinced him otherwise—either in an attempt to win favor with the girls or, as the sisters thought more likely, so she could have extra time alone with her future husband.

Connor shrugged in response to Ling's question. "Fifty percent. It was more a *gut feeling*."

"You know how unlikely this is," she said, sipping from a can of Diet Coke she'd gotten from the snack bar. "I mean, we're thousands of miles away from Sydney, virtually on the other side of the world."

"I realize that," Connor replied, beginning to doubt his own eyes. "I just wish you'd been there to ID him."

Ling held up her hands. "Hey, I was busy fending off the boys swarming around Chloe."

"You weren't doing too badly yourself," Connor remarked, nudging her with his elbow.

Ling narrowed her eyes at him. "*He* was talking to *me*. I was still in Code Yellow. Anyway, have you reported your sighting to Brad or the captain yet?"

"No," Connor admitted. "You remember what Bugsy taught us: *Once is happenstance, twice is circumstance. Three times means enemy action.* Unless I see that man again, the sighting means nothing."

Ling pursed her lips. "Well, Chloe seems to be getting into the full swing of the party."

Over the portable speakers Bob Marley's "Could You Be Loved" pulsed its summery lilting beat. Chloe was dancing with a boy in Bermuda shorts. Although not wanting to intrude on her fun, Connor realized they'd have to keep a close eye on her. Meanwhile, Emily sat by the fire, chatting with two girls and a red-haired boy who was showing a clear interest in her. But Connor didn't judge him a threat. He was half his size and, by the looks of it, getting nowhere with Emily.

As Connor surveyed the party, a tall boy with curly sun-bleached hair swaggered over to them.

"Hey!" he drawled.

"Hi, Dave," Ling replied, offering a friendly yet reserved smile. Connor recognized him as the boy who'd been speaking with her earlier that afternoon.

"What you doing over here? The party's happening over *there*." Dave wafted his arm in the general direction of the music.

"There's a better view from here," replied Ling.

"Really?" Dave turned his head and looked for himself.

Ling rolled her eyes at Connor, the boy having no idea what she actually meant by this. From their position outside the party, the two of them occupied the best surveillance point. They could see the beach, the bonfire and the snack bar. Their two Principals were always under their watchful guard yet had the freedom to enjoy themselves without Connor or Ling constantly at their side. And by not being too close to the fire, they kept some of their night vision, meaning people didn't suddenly materialize out of the darkness.

"Seems good to me wherever you look," said Dave, gazing directly at Ling. "Especially this way."

He flumped down in the sand beside her and offered her an open-topped coconut with a straw sticking out.

"No thanks," said Ling, her terse tone making it clear that Dave should rejoin his friends in the dance circle.

"Suit yourself!" said Dave, taking a slurp. He jutted his chin toward Connor. "He your boyfriend?"

Ling glanced at Connor and smirked. "No, I have taste."

Dave broke into a broad grin. "Didn't think so." He bent forward to catch Connor's eye. "No offense, man."

"None taken," replied Connor, wondering when the boy would realize he wasn't welcome.

But Dave was clearly determined to continue chatting with Ling, talking about his surfing prowess earlier that day. Tuning out from the conversation, Connor's eyes swept the party again. Chloe was now jumping up and down to "Happy" by Pharrell Williams. Her sister had joined her, and the red-haired boy from the bonfire was dancing alongside them both.

As he observed the dancers, he caught sight of a tattooed arm in the firelight. His alert status went from Code Yellow to Code Orange. *Focused awareness.* His eyes searched among the partygoers for another glimpse. But, outside the glow of the fire, the beach was too dark to make out any individual beyond their silhouettes. The next pool of light was the snack bar with its glistening oil lamps.

Then Connor saw a flash of a muscled bicep with a roaring lion tattoo.

40

"Ling, I think I just saw Todd," said Connor, interrupting Dave's surf monologue.

Ling turned to him, a frown on her face. "Todd?"

"*Yes*, Todd Logan," Connor repeated, giving her a pointed look. "You remember, the Rollerblader."

"So, the wave pulled me under. I thought I was gonna be *fish food* . . ." continued Dave, trying desperately to keep Ling's attention. But she ignored his ramblings as the name's full significance hit home.

"Where?" Ling demanded, her eyes sharp as she hunted the darkness.

"Over there, by the dancers."

Ling craned her neck. "I can't see him. Are you sure?"

"I didn't see his face," admitted Connor, "but I recognized his lion tattoo."

Ling leaned over to Connor and whispered, "We can't

simply extract the girls from the party just because you saw a tattoo. It could just be a random tourist with a similar tattoo and we'd end up spoiling everyone's night, on the basis of a suspicion."

A memory surfaced in Connor's mind of the mishap at the school dance last year with Alicia. In his haste to act and protect her, he'd inadvertently ruined her evening and nearly brought his first mission to an abrupt end.

But then he thought about all the times when his instincts had been spot-on, and he decided to trust them once again.

"It's too much of a coincidence to ignore," he insisted. "We can't take the risk."

"Okay," relented Ling, getting to her feet. "Then we need to eyeball him first. Get confirmation."

Dave looked up with a slightly forlorn expression. "Hey, Ling. Forget Todd. Think Dave!"

"In another life," replied Ling over her shoulder as she and Connor strode toward the main party.

"Let's split up," Connor suggested, "but stay in comms."

Ling nodded in agreement, and they both inserted their covert earpieces.

"*Alpha One to Alpha Two. Comms check,*" whispered Connor.

"I'm standing right next to you, idiot!" hissed Ling. "But I hear you loud and clear. Now you take left flank and I'll take right."

The two of them circled around the mass of people raving on the beach. The music was pumping, and in the flame-lit darkness the dancers became a tangle of bare arms and legs, faces shifting in and out of view, making it hard to identify anyone. But, as he worked his way through the party, Connor kept a visual lock on Emily and Chloe's position.

"Have you spotted him yet?" came Ling's voice in his ear.

"Negative," replied Connor.

A pretty girl swayed to the music in front of him, trying to catch his eye. He smiled at her. At any other time, he'd leap at such an opportunity, but there were more important matters at stake right now. He edged past her, heading in the direction of the bar.

Above the music he suddenly heard Chloe's voice shout, "CONNOR!"

He spun around, his heart in his mouth at the anticipated sight of her being dragged away into the darkness. But she was just bouncing up and down, waving for him to join her in a dance. Breathing once more, Connor pointed in the direction of the bathroom. Chloe gave him the thumbs-up in understanding and returned to her dancing. On the opposite side of the dancers, Ling continued with her surveillance sweep. She made eye contact with him.

"Any sign?" she asked.

Connor shook his head.

"Maybe you were mistaken."

"No, I'm sure I saw—" At that moment, Connor noticed movement behind the palm-thatched snack bar, a figure lurking out of sight from all the other partygoers.

"I've spotted him," he whispered. "Behind the snack bar."

"Are you sure?" said Ling, altering course toward the building.

Using the palm trees for cover, Connor moved in for a definite confirmation. The man had his back to him. He couldn't be certain. He crept to within a few feet of his target. Then he saw, in the reflected glow of an oil lamp, the tattoo.

"It's Todd!" whispered Connor into his mic.

"Watch out," cried Ling as the figure turned toward Connor's voice. *"He's got a machete."*

A gleam of steel flashed in the lamplight, the vicious blade slicing through the air. Connor leaped aside as Ling ran up behind and launched into a flying side kick. Her foot struck the man's back, sending him sprawling into the sand. Kicking away his machete, Connor grabbed his arm and twisted it into a lock. Ling seized the other arm, rotating it until the wrist threatened to snap.

"Ow! Help!" he cried, writhing on the ground in agony.

"Don't struggle or I'll break your wrist," Ling hissed.

"What the hell is going on here?" shouted a gruff voice from behind. "Leave my employee alone!"

As the snack bar manager stormed over, Connor and Ling stared at the man they had pinned to the ground. Although tattooed and dark-haired, he was *not* Todd Logan. Only now, up close, could Connor see that the tattoo wasn't a roaring lion. It was a tiger.

41

"Well done, hotshot!" said Ling, her tone dripping with sarcasm as the two of them, having made their apologies to the man with the tiger tattoo, beat a hasty retreat to the party.

"Sorry, it was dark, I couldn't see his face," Connor replied. "And he *did* have a machete."

"To cut coconuts with."

"But *you* were the one who jumped him," argued Connor.

Ling spun on him and jabbed a finger in his chest. "Don't blame me for your mistakes! I'm always having to pick up the slack on this mission."

"What do you mean?"

Ling let out a derisive snort and fixed him with a withering look. "Well, to start with, on Manly Beach you completely failed to spot that mugger's approach. And I had to keep him from escaping with *your* Principal's handbag."

"That was Jason's fault," explained Connor. "If he hadn't—"

"Don't bring Jason into this," said Ling, cutting him off.

"Your reactions were slow and you know it. And what about the other day? I believe it was *me* who noticed *your* Principal floating off on an inflatable mattress. I thought you were supposed to be a gold-winged guardian. Now you're seeing threats where there aren't any!"

Connor held up his hands in surrender. "Okay, you're right. I realize I've made some mistakes. That's probably why I'm being so jumpy, but I know what I s—"

"Hang on," Ling interrupted. "Where's Emily?"

For the second time that night, Connor felt his throat tighten in panic. He scanned the crowd for Emily's face, but everyone kept moving and twirling, the dark and firelight confusing the scene. Then he spotted the red-haired boy dancing with— "No, it's *Chloe* that's missing," corrected Connor.

"Are you sure?" said Ling, squinting at the remaining sister.

"Yes, that boy hasn't left Emily's side all night."

Ling cursed. "Chloe could be pretty much *anywhere*," she muttered as she hunted the darkness for her Principal.

Connor didn't like the situation either. Beyond the glow of the bonfire lay a one-mile stretch of starlit beach. It would be virtually impossible to find her, especially near the tree line where the darkness was absolute.

They did a sweep of the party, down toward the bonfire. When this didn't produce a result, Connor checked his watch. Chloe had been missing at least five minutes, long enough to start getting concerned. He approached Emily in the crowd. She greeted him with an unexpected kiss on the cheek.

"Have you come to save me from this boy?" she whispered in his ear, flicking her eyes toward her dance partner. The boy frowned at Connor, clearly wondering why he was intruding.

"Sorry, man," said Connor with an apologetic smile. "We have to go."

Connor led Emily away by the hand, leaving the boy openmouthed and crestfallen.

"Thanks," said Emily. "He was sweet, but a real bore."

"Do you know where your sister is?" Connor asked, getting straight to the point.

Emily shrugged. "She said she was going to the bathroom."

Connor relayed this information to Ling.

"I've already checked. She's not there," came Ling's tense reply in his ear.

They regrouped at the edge of the party, Connor keeping Emily close. If her sister was missing, then he couldn't afford to let Emily out of his sight. There might be a completely innocent explanation for Chloe's disappearance. However, the longer she was gone, the less chance the outcome would be good. She could have wandered off with a boy, whose intentions might or might not be honorable. She could have gone swimming and been caught in a current, or fallen over in the darkness and hurt herself. Or maybe he *had* seen Todd, as well as his accomplice earlier that day in the forest, and the two men had snatched her. The nightmare scenarios were endless.

"What should we do?" said Ling, a hint of desperation edging her voice.

Connor realized he had to take charge of the situation. Definitive action was the best solution to such an emergency. "First, we call Brad to bring the tender over," he said, pulling out his phone. "We can't search the beach and protect Emily at the same time."

Once he'd spoken with Brad and explained the situation, Emily asked, "Do you think my sister's okay?"

She eyed the darkness fearfully as if invisible hands would reach out and spirit her away too. Connor wore his most reassuring smile. "I'm sure she is. But we can't take any risks. I'm sending you back to the *Orchid* while we look for her."

"Hey! I thought you were leaving."

The three of them turned to see the red-haired boy approaching, a hurt expression on his face.

Emily nodded. "We are, but we have to find my sister first."

"Well, I just saw her." The boy pointed up the beach. "She's in the snack bar with Matt."

"*What?*" exclaimed Ling. "I must have walked straight past her."

The three of them hurried up to the snack bar, leaving Emily's admirer behind again.

"Does that mean you're staying now?" the boy called out hopefully, getting no reply.

They found Chloe perched on a stool, chin resting in the palm of her hand as she gazed into the dark eyes of the boy with Bermuda shorts. Matt had broad shoulders, a six-pack and an easygoing smile. A few years older than Chloe, he had clearly charmed her.

"Well, panic over," said Emily, sighing with visible relief.

"I still think it's time to go," Ling said to Connor, her eyes flicking toward Matt, who had an eager look on his face. She strode determinedly over to the snack bar and broke up the intimate twosome. "Sorry, but we have to leave now."

Chloe's jaw dropped. "But the party isn't over yet!"

"Brad's on his way. Besides, your father said to bring you home before eleven."

Chloe looked mortified, her cheeks flushing with a mix of embarrassment and rage. *"Just leave us alone,"* she hissed.

Ling stood her ground. "No can do."

"Oh, don't be such a killjoy!" said Chloe, waving her off. "Look, if you're worried about my safety, don't be. Matt can protect me."

"Sure I can," he said, resting a hand on Chloe's arm while offering Ling a winning smile.

Ling remained unmoved by his charm. "You don't get a hungry lion to protect a lamb."

Matt's brow knotted in confusion. "Say again?"

"Oh, forget it," said Ling, losing patience with him. "We have to go."

Chloe glared at her, refusing to shift from her stool. After several moments of uncomfortable silence, Matt held up his hands. "Listen, I can see I'm causing problems." He turned to Chloe. "I'll catch you another time."

"But we might be sailing to another island tomorrow!" she protested.

Matt glanced uneasily at the small yet forceful Chinese girl standing beside him. "I think it's for the best if you do go."

Chloe fumed at Ling. "Well, *at least* give me a chance to say good-bye."

"Certainly," replied Ling, turning on her heel and rejoining Connor and Emily.

She raised her eyebrows at Connor and tutted in exasperation. Connor shrugged sympathetically, although he thought Ling could have handled the situation a little more tactfully.

They waited while Chloe enveloped Matt in a hug and kissed him on both cheeks. When she finally released him, he grinned and winked at her. Chloe then made her way out of the bar.

She threw Ling a scathing look. "Thanks for nothing, I was just starting to enjoy myself."

"Yes, it *sure* looked like it," replied Ling.

"What are you implying? Matt's a nice guy."

"How do you know?" challenged Ling.

Chloe stared at her in disbelief. "You don't trust boys very much, do you?"

"No," replied Ling, leading her toward the jetty. "Especially ones I don't know."

42

"What a night!" said Ling, collapsing in one of the recliners on the *Orchid*'s foredeck. The area was secluded from the rest of the yacht and little used by the Sterling family, who preferred the more spacious and wind-sheltered living quarters toward the stern.

Lying back in the adjacent recliner, Connor gazed in awe at the galaxy of stars overhead. He'd never seen so many in his life. Unobscured by clouds or light pollution, the sky seemed dusted with glimmering diamonds.

"Well, we survived and both Principals are safe," he replied, making himself comfortable.

"Yeah, no thanks to Chloe," muttered Ling. "Look, I'm sorry about what I said to you earlier."

"Not a problem. I deserved it." Connor glanced over at Ling. "But Chloe was only enjoying herself."

Ling tsked. "Well, you would take her side, wouldn't you?"

"What's that supposed to mean?"

Ling rolled her eyes. "Boys! She has you wrapped around her little finger. *Oh, Connor, I need your protection,*" she mocked in Chloe's voice, waving a pretend bottle of suntan lotion at him.

Connor brushed off her jibe. "Come on, you must admit you were a little heavy-handed with her tonight."

Ling huffed. "She shouldn't have gone off on her own in the first place. But it's not just that. She's a huge pain in the neck. She treats me like her personal slave. Expects me to carry her bags, get her drinks, pick up her clothes. And she never listens when I try to give her safety advice. Doesn't she understand that my job is to protect her, not *serve* her?"

Connor's eye caught a shooting star trace its way across the sky. "You should cut Chloe some slack. She's never had a bodyguard before, so she probably doesn't know what we're actually supposed to do."

"Well, Emily seems to understand. And there's no reason to be rude or bossy about it. I'm sorry, but I don't find it easy to sympathize with people who have everything."

"Don't forget their mother died in a car crash, one of them's been kidnapped and their father's too busy with work, or his fiancée, to spend any time with them. They don't exactly have an easy life."

"Well, their life isn't exactly tough either," countered Ling, indicating the multimillion-dollar super-yacht.

Connor thought about his own situation. His gran had

always said, "Wealth is empty; it's family that fills the heart." He looked at Ling. "Money doesn't necessarily mean happiness."

"Yeah, but it sure helps," said Ling, staring hard at Connor. "I'll tell you what tough is. I grew up as a street kid in Shanghai. It was survival of the strongest and meanest. I had nothing apart from my wits to live on. And as a *girl* I was at an immediate disadvantage. I used to live in a cardboard box down an alleyway."

Connor stared at Ling in shock at this sudden revelation.

"The only good thing about it was the kung fu club in a nearby basement. I'd spy on their lessons through a grating in the wall, teaching myself the moves. It wasn't exactly an *easy* life. I had stomach cramps on the days I couldn't scavenge food. But the kung fu kept my mind off it. The *shifu* used to say, 'It's hard to beat a person who never gives up.' I lived by that mantra every miserable day of my life on those streets."

Connor was speechless. He'd had no clue about Ling's troubled past. Did anyone else in Alpha team know? At least now he understood what the colonel had meant by her "tough" background, and it partly explained Ling's constant need to prove herself.

"How did you ever become a guardian?" he asked.

"Colonel Black caught me picking his pocket."

Connor sat up in surprise. "Doing *what*?"

Ling knitted her fingers behind her head, grinning at the memory. "Yeah, I almost got away with it too. But at the last second the colonel grabbed my wrist and put me in a lock. Not that it stopped me. I simply spun out of it, kicked him in the knee and ran. But he was with Steve, our combat instructor, at the time. Gee, was he fast! He cornered me in an alley. I thought I'd be beaten within an inch of my life, but rather than punish me or turn me over to the police, the colonel *recruited* me."

Connor was stunned. "Why did he do that?"

Ling shrugged. "Said he was impressed with my stealth and fighting spirit. Being streetwise, he thought I had the makings of a bodyguard." Ling laughed. "Anyway, the colonel arranged a passport and a visa for me, and I ended up at Guardian HQ. The rest is history."

She looked at Connor and narrowed her eyes thoughtfully. "I do sometimes wonder, though, whether he *let* me pick his pocket."

Recalling his own recruitment, the corner of Connor's mouth curled into a smile. "Sounds like the colonel's tactics to me."

43

Connor looked at his watch. "Time to do our final security sweep."

"Yep, better make sure the princesses are safely tucked into bed!" quipped Ling, hauling herself out of the recliner.

Connor switched on his flashlight, the bright beam shining off the smooth wooden deck. They headed aft along the port side of the yacht. All the crew members were in their quarters, except one of the deckhands, Scott, who was on official watch duty on the bridge. There was no real need for an additional security check, yet since Brad had said the more eyeballs the better, Connor thought it couldn't do any harm.

With the girls having gone to their cabins and Mr. Sterling and his fiancée tucked away in their personal suite, all was quiet on board. Only the lapping of the sea against the hull and the distant beat of music from the beach intruded on the tropical night's peace. Connor could see the bonfire burning on the shore, its glow reflected in the rippling waters of the bay.

As the two of them reached the stern and headed back up the starboard side, Connor wondered if they'd overreacted to Chloe's "disappearance." It wasn't as if she'd been gone long, nor had she gone far. In hindsight, they could have spent a bit more time *looking* before jumping to the wrong conclusion. It was certainly a sign of their inexperience as guardians, but Brad had been kind in his appraisal. He considered they'd made the right decision, saying it was better to act on a potential threat and be wrong than ignore it and find out to their detriment that the threat was real.

"Look! The crew's left the gangway down again," said Ling, pointing to the steel steps leading up from the waterline. "I thought Brad warned them about that."

She pressed the button to retract the gangway. As they waited for it to whirr quietly back into its recess, Connor's flashlight caught a gleam on the deck. He looked closer. It was a damp footprint. Fresh.

He widened the arc of his beam and more footprints appeared, leading away into the darkness.

"One of the crew?" suggested Ling.

"Swimming at this time of night?" said Connor, shaking his head dubiously.

They followed the trail to the first flight of external steps. Silently ascending to the upper deck, Connor felt a growing disquiet at the thought of an intruder on board. Brad had informed them about a spate of thefts that had occurred on yachts docked at Victoria Harbor and the surrounding bays, but those boats hadn't generally been occupied at the time.

Peering around the final step, they saw no one on the upper deck at first. Then Ling spotted a shadowy figure spying through a window into the VIP guest room.

"I think we should get Brad," whispered Connor.

"Too late for that," replied Ling as the intruder opened the door leading to the suite. Chloe was standing on the other side. The intruder grabbed her. She squealed.

"Quiet!" he hissed, his hand over her mouth.

Without waiting a second longer, Ling leaped up and ran full speed at the intruder.

"Let her go!" she cried, kicking at the attacker's knee from behind.

His balance broken, he toppled backward. Ling seized his hair in one hand and his chin in the other, then twisted his head and pushed down. But, rather than guiding the intruder to the deck, she launched him over the rail.

Where the head goes, the body follows, Connor recalled their combat instructor saying when he'd first taught them the "head-twist" technique.

Screaming, the intruder somersaulted through the air and splashed into the sea.

"What did you do *that* for?" Chloe cried, her jaw dropping open in shock and horror.

Ling stared in bafflement at her Principal. "He was attacking you."

"He was my *guest*! That was Matt you just threw overboard."

"Oh!" said Ling, putting a hand to her mouth. Connor couldn't quite tell if it was to hide her embarrassment at the mistake or her amusement.

"Well, you know, we can't just let anyone on board," said Ling in her own defense. "It's a security risk."

Chloe threw up her hands in despair. "You are a *nightmare!*" she cried before slamming the door in Ling's face.

44

Ruth McArthur lit her second cigarette of the night. Exhaling a puff of acrid smoke, she watched it rise to the grime-stained ceiling of the pedestrian underpass running beneath Manning Road on the University of Sydney campus. The fluorescent strip lights, naked and harsh, cast a sickly glow onto the colorful scene surrounding her. The walls, the ceiling, and even the floor were infected with a profusion of graffiti and tags, as if the tunnel itself were bleeding paint. Cutting through the smog of her cigarette, the lingering fumes from aerosol cans filled Ruth's nostrils and made her slightly nauseated.

Yet as editor in chief of Sterling's flagship paper, *Australian Daily*, she'd experienced her fair share of war zones, drug dens and slums. This particular location didn't spook her at all. Not that this meant she was naive. She kept a firm grip on her car keys in one hand, a tip she'd learned from self-defense lessons. The protruding metal points made an effective improvised weapon if the situation demanded it.

The tunnel was deserted, the silence almost echoing in on itself. In these late hours of the night, the only life passing through would be the occasional tagger or graffiti artist wanting to make their mark.

Ruth glanced at her watch, beginning to wonder if her contact from the government's Department of Resources and Energy would show. Acquiring information on the Harry Gibb case had been like getting blood from a stone. No one seemed to want to pursue any other line of inquiry than death by natural causes. Case closed. But her inside contact claimed to have proof otherwise.

Stamping out her cigarette, Ruth reached into her bag for her phone. Her contact might have left a message. She thumbed in her password, but there were no missed calls, and her inbox was empty. One of the strip lights flickered and buzzed overhead, dimming the passageway momentarily. She glanced up and had to stifle a scream in her throat. Where there had been just shadow now stood a man in a gray suit. She had not heard or seen his approach, and it was as if the man had materialized straight out of the graffiti, leaching all color in the process.

"Ruth McArthur?" the man said, his voice dry and somehow soulless.

"Yes," she said, unclenching the keys in her fist. This must be her contact. "And you are . . . James?"

The man was older than Ruth expected, yet at the same time strangely ageless. *Like a well-preserved corpse,* she thought, before shuddering away the unsettling image in her mind.

"You want to know about Harry Gibb?" he said.

Ruth nodded.

The man glanced up and down the tunnel. "You're not an undercover cop or federal agent, are you?"

"No, of course not." Ruth produced her press ID.

He studied her photo and credentials. "Press passes can easily be faked."

Ruth appreciated the reason for her contact's wariness. The fallout from Harry Gibb's corrupt dealings was catastrophic for the current government. Many in power had been glad of the politician's death and were hoping the scandal would be buried along with him. But Ruth had caught the scent of a bigger story, a far wider and more sinister conspiracy, and she wanted to know the truth. She sensed this might be the journalistic scoop of her career.

"Well, how about I tell you what I think happened? Then you can just confirm or deny it," she suggested.

The man neither nodded nor shook his head, so she continued, "My theory is that Harry Gibb was murdered. Or to put it more accurately, assassinated."

There was a barely perceptible twitch of his eyebrow. "You have proof of this?"

"No, nothing concrete," admitted Ruth. "I was hoping you could provide that."

"How did you come to this conclusion about Harry when the cops didn't?"

"I'm a journalist. I always look more deeply than the police. I get the sense that something's missing. Literally, in this case. Harry had known heart problems. When I spoke with his secretary, she told me that he always kept a bottle of beta-blockers in his desk drawer. But there was no bottle there or anywhere at the scene. That I consider suspicious."

The man nodded. "Suspicious, but not conclusive. What else have you discovered?"

Ruth didn't usually give so much away during an interview with a contact, but she needed to win his trust. "Well, his PC's hard drive was secure-wiped to a zero state. The accepted truth was that Harry did that to cover his tracks. But a malware virus, linked to his computer, infiltrated the rest of the office network. The IT technician said he'd seen nothing like it. The virus was highly advanced, targeting specific keywords and files and leaving holes throughout their system, despite multiple firewalls and antivirus software. In his opinion, it smacked of governmental espionage. Then there's the missing physical file from the archives."

The man took a step closer. "You know about the missing file?"

Ruth nodded. She was *definitely* onto something. "It took me a while to discover it. On that day, the building security camera malfunctioned. Yet a digital record showed that Harry had accessed the archive room ten minutes before his death. A folder labeled MINING RIGHTS, GOLDFIELDS, WA, was logged in the filing system but wasn't there when I looked. However, I did find this at the bottom of the cabinet."

Ruth produced a slip of crumpled paper from her bag. "It lists investment amounts and sources, although I'm not sure how useful it is, since a number of the companies don't actually exist—"

"Have you made a copy of that?" interrupted her contact.

"No . . ." began Ruth, frowning. "Look, it should be me asking *you* the questions. I was led to believe you had evidence relating to Harry's murder."

A flicker of a smile registered on her contact's lean face, almost too fast and certainly too cold to pass off as a real smile. "That I do. You're right on all counts. Harry was assassinated."

Ruth's eyes lit up. She had her story. "By whom?"

"One of his investors."

"Which one? As I said, most of the ones listed here were shell companies. Unless you mean"—she held up the piece of paper and smiled slyly—"the organization behind them?"

The man's eyes became glacial. "What information do you have on this organization?"

Ruth suddenly felt uneasy in his presence. She tightened her grip on her car keys.

"Tell me," said the man, seizing her arm and preventing Ruth from using her "weapon."

"Let me go!" demanded Ruth.

"No, not until you tell me."

The man's fingers dug deep into her flesh, finding a nerve point and sending a spasm of pain through her.

"Not much," Ruth admitted through teeth clenched in agony. "There were only ghost trails from the false companies. I know it goes by the name of Equilibrium and has interests in everything from oil to water to mining. But for what purpose I can't quite fathom. The company isn't registered on any stock exchange."

"Who else have you told?" He tightened his grip on her arm.

"No one. I've only just discovered it for myself."

He released her arm, the pain instantly subsiding. "Good. Equilibrium is a dangerous organization to know."

Ruth rubbed her arm. Her contact was clearly paranoid as well as unpredictable. "Listen, if you're worried for your own safety, then I know people who can help protect you."

The man laughed, hollow and cruel. "No one is safe from Equilibrium."

"Well then, if you have proof they're connected to Harry's

murder, perhaps we can draw out this organization. Expose them."

The man gave a long considered sigh. "Ruth, you certainly deserve your reputation for investigative journalism."

He reached into his jacket pocket and pulled out a fountain pen. "I have someone you should talk to. Who can explain everything," he said, slowly removing the top of the pen. "Do you have a notepad? I'll write his contact number down for you."

"Yes, of course." Ruth scrabbled inside her handbag. She wanted to end this meeting as quickly as possible.

Only as she was retrieving her notepad did she notice the peculiar shape of the pen. The tip itself was a long sharp needle, far too thin for writing. In the split second that she registered this oddity, the point sank into the soft flesh of her neck. A liquid fire coursed through her veins, the agonizing shock smothering all attempts to cry out. The lurid graffiti of the tunnel swirled rapidly into blackness and she slumped to the floor, followed by the soft jangle of keys.

45

"The fault lay with a distorted gasket in the fuel system," explained Amir, his face bright on the screen of Connor's laptop.

"Well, that makes me rest easier at night!" replied Ling, who sat on the bed with Connor for the morning's video briefing with Alpha team. "I have literally no idea what you're talking about."

"A gasket is a mechanical seal that prevents leakage while under compression—"

"Thanks, Amir, but such detail isn't required," Charley cut in, appearing on the screen beside him. "The important point is that the Seychelles coast guard discovered the cause of the Jet Ski explosion."

"We saw the pictures," said Richie, his grinning face butting in front of Amir's. "That Jet Ski was totaled! Luckily it wasn't one of the sisters riding it. That could have been disastrous—"

"Hang on: *I* was on it!" exclaimed Ling, her expression indignant.

"Yeah, I know, but you're tough enough," replied Richie.

He was suddenly yanked out of the frame and Jason's bulk appeared. "Ignore that Irish idiot. How are you doing, Ling?"

"Fine," she replied, clearly pleased to see him. "To be honest, my Principal's more of a pain than the burn."

Jason laughed. "I'm afraid that goes with the territory of being a guardian. On my last assignment, I could've throttled my Principal!"

"Sorry to break up the happy reunion," said Charley, "but we need to focus on this Jet Ski situation."

Jason nodded. "Stay cool, Ling," he said, giving her a wink before slipping out of view.

"Joking aside, Ling, you were extremely lucky to have survived the explosion," continued Charley. "Without your protective clothing, you could have been seriously injured or even killed."

Ling nonchalantly lay back on one of the pillows. "All part of the job, isn't it?"

"No, it isn't," said Charley firmly, shifting in her wheelchair. "Or at least with the right security in place, it shouldn't be."

Connor sensed Charley's own experience in that statement, but this wasn't the time or place to delve into her past. "So the explosion was just an accident?" he asked.

Charley pensively bit her lower lip. "That's one way of looking at it. Brad's report, however, said that the *Orchid's* engineer had checked the other Jet Ski and discovered a similar issue with its fuel-filler inlet. It too could have very easily exploded."

Connor and Ling exchanged uneasy glances. Connor turned back to the laptop's webcam. "Are you suggesting *sabotage?*"

"We can't rule that possibility out. It may just be a manu-facturing defect. It does happen. But on *both* Jet Skis? That's why we must assume this was an attempt on the lives of the Sterling family, designed to look like an accident."

"So, who might have done it?" asked Ling.

"Your guess is as good as ours at this time. The last person known to have touched the Jet Skis was the engineer, but Brad questioned him and vouches for his integrity. So it remains to be seen . . ." Charley looked offscreen. "Hang on, Colonel Black's here."

Charley and Amir moved aside so the colonel could sit in front of the webcam. His jaw was set, and his gray eyes were hard as flint.

"I've just been speaking with Mr. Sterling. Ling, you're being pulled off Operation Gemini, effective immediately."

46

"Why am I taking the flak for something *she* did wrong?" Ling asked, shoving her clothes into her bag with such force, the seams threatened to split.

Connor stood by her cabin door, arms crossed, as Ling vented her fury on her packing.

"I mean, I was just trying to protect her. And what thanks do I get? None. I might as well walk the plank."

"You made Matt do that," Connor remarked.

Pausing a moment, Ling smirked. "Yeah, I suppose I did. Well, he shouldn't have been on board anyway." She resumed her fierce packing. "Now the colonel won't trust me on another operation for months!"

"The colonel's not stupid. He knows the score. Don't forget, I was thrown off my first operation."

Ling glanced up and gave a halfhearted laugh. "I forgot about that, hotshot. Maybe I'll get to save the day too. Know any terrorists or presidents' daughters in the Seychelles?"

Connor gently shook his head. "Look, what I'm trying to say is that it doesn't matter."

"Not to you maybe, but I have to go back to Alpha team with my tail between my legs."

Brad stuck his head into the cabin. "The tender's ready."

"Good," said Ling as she grabbed the last of her stuff. "I can't wait to get off this stinking ship."

"Hey! Lightning Ling," said Brad, clamping a hand on her shoulder and giving it a squeeze. "For what it's worth, I think you were doing a stellar job."

Ling looked up into Brad's craggy face. "Then why am I being dismissed?"

"Bodyguards and their Principals can be as close as bread and butter . . . or fight like cats and dogs. Sometimes there's simply a clash of personalities. I've had such moments in my career. You just need to roll with the punches."

"I'll roll her with a punch," muttered Ling, sealing up the bag and heading for the door.

Brad raised his eyebrows at Connor, and the two of them followed Ling up to the main deck.

"Aren't we risking the girls' safety by losing Ling?" asked Connor quietly.

"The colonel and I both voiced our concerns to Mr. Sterling," replied Brad. "But he's adamant Ling must go. I'm not happy with it. But, since the girls won't be leaving the yacht before Ling's replacement arrives, I can't foresee any real problems.

You'll just have to work double shifts!" he added with a wink.

At the top of the lowered gangway, Ling stopped. "Well, Connor, it's been a blast."

"Literally," said Connor, thinking of the Jet Ski.

Ling laughed. "How are you ever going to survive without me?"

Connor shrugged. "It's only four days. And we're at sea the whole time. Besides, the colonel's sending Luciana from Bravo team to join me in the Maldives."

"Good luck to her! She'll need it."

"What do you mean by that? Protecting Chloe or working with me?" said Connor, feigning offense.

Ling punched him on the arm. "You're all right, Connor. If a little jumpy." She started down the steps to the tender. "I'll catch you back at HQ. Just don't strain yourself putting too much suntan lotion on the girls."

Brad started the engine. He was to drop off Ling in Baie Sainte Anne, where she would take a catamaran to the main island and catch a plane home. However, as they were about to leave, Mr. Sterling appeared.

"Hold up, Brad. Change of plan."

They all turned to him in surprise. Was Ling getting a last-minute reprieve? But Mr. Sterling's expression was too grave for that hope.

47

"I can't believe our father just up and left like that!" said Chloe, perched on the edge of the hot tub, her legs dangling in the bubbling water.

"We haven't seen much of him anyway," Emily muttered as she took a photo of Mahé Island receding into the distance.

Chloe glanced over the rail at the occupied sun bed in the sky lounge below. "I just wish he'd taken Amanda with him."

Connor sat quietly at the dining table on the sundeck. It wasn't his place to voice his opinion. Mr. Sterling had informed his daughters that Ruth McArthur, his editor in chief, had been killed in a suspected mugging incident and that he had to interrupt his vacation to manage the fallout at the newspaper. The yacht had been rerouted via the main island to drop off Mr. Sterling and his bodyguard, along with the disgraced Ling, at the airport. Captain Locke had then set a course for the Maldives, where Mr. Sterling hoped to rejoin them in a week's time.

"I wouldn't worry," said Emily, pocketing her phone. "This boat's big enough for all of us. And she'll probably sunbathe the entire time." She screwed her eyes shut and rubbed her temples.

"Are you all right?" asked Connor.

"Yeah, it's just a headache. I get them a lot. I think it's my medication." Emily headed over to the stairs. "I'm going to take a nap. See you at dinner."

Connor offered her a sympathetic smile but remained at the table. There was no reason to shadow her while on board. They were in coastal waters, the yacht was cruising at a sedate speed, and he and Brad had performed a security sweep before departing Mahé. The threat level was low.

Reaching into his polo-shirt pocket, Connor pulled out his phone. Its orange neoprene cover was still annoyingly bulky, but the waterproofing had been a godsend when he'd dived into the sea to rescue Ling after the Jet-Ski explosion. Unlocking the screen, he messaged his mum and gran to let them know everything was okay, taking the opportunity before the *Orchid* entered the open ocean and they lost the signal altogether. Then he reached for his book and settled back into his chair.

"Come and join me," said Chloe as she immersed herself fully in the hot tub.

Connor glanced over. He was more wary of her since Ling's unwarranted dismissal. "Thank you, but no."

Chloe sighed. "Don't be angry with me. I realize Ling was your friend, but she was really getting on my nerves."

"She was just doing her job," Connor replied, not wanting to get into a discussion.

"I realize that, but I couldn't do a single thing without her intervening or making some comment. It was *suffocating*. It's my sister who needs the protection, not me."

Connor shook his head. He recognized that Ling's manner might have been abrasive and heavy-handed, but there were genuine threats to the girls' lives. "I'm afraid you're wrong. *Both* of you are potential targets."

"That's my sister's fault," muttered Chloe. "I can't have any fun because of her. Ever since she was kidnapped, my dad has virtually grounded me. I haven't been able to hang out alone with friends or go to the beach or even shop on my own. Do you know how claustrophobic that feels? This vacation is the *first* time I've been allowed any freedom in over a year."

"Your father only wants to protect you," responded Connor. "That intruder last night could have been a kidnapper, an assassin or worse."

"But it was only Matt," said Chloe, dismissing the suggestion with a wave of her hand. "The point is, my father allows me no freedom at home, and puts me under so much pressure to succeed at school that I *need* to let off some steam. Otherwise I'll go stir-crazy."

Connor noticed tears of frustration welling up in Chloe's eyes and felt a touch of sympathy for her situation. It wasn't her choice to have twenty-four-hour security.

"Fair enough," he relented. "Look, when we get to the Maldives, I'll speak with Luciana and we'll work out a way to give you some freedom without compromising your safety."

Chloe's face lit up. "Thanks, you're a star. Now are you going to join me or not?"

"Best not," replied Connor. "I'm on duty."

"You're *always* on duty." She crossed her arms on the side of the hot tub and stared at him. "As I understand, you're now *my* guardian until the Maldives. So, as your Principal, I say you need to relax. That was Ling's problem; don't make it yours."

Connor inwardly sighed. He knew he was being manipulated, but he didn't want to upset her either. An uncooperative Principal was a liability. Putting down his book, he took off his polo shirt and then thought better of it.

Chloe's hopeful smile waned as he pulled the shirt back over his head. "What's the problem?"

"Nothing," he replied. Although he guessed a dip in the hot tub wouldn't be crossing any lines as a guardian, his actions could be easily misinterpreted, and he didn't want to have to explain himself to Charley a second time.

As he put his arm through the sleeve, Chloe spotted the slim white scar on his left shoulder. "What happened there?"

"Knife wound," he said, pulling up the collar.

Her eyes widened with a mix of concern and fascination. "Did you get that while protecting someone?"

Connor nodded.

"Did it hurt?"

"Yes, but I didn't have much time to think about it. I was in the middle of a fight, trying to escape."

Chloe sat up, studying his face with admiration. "You must have been really brave."

Connor shook his head. "I didn't have much choice in the matter."

"So . . . do you like my sister?" she asked.

Caught completely off guard, Connor replied, "Yes, of course"—then he saw Chloe frown—"but not that way. As guardians, we have to remain strictly friends with any Principal."

"Really?" Biting at her lower lip, Chloe gazed intently at him. "That must be very difficult at times, I mean, to remain *just* friends. Haven't you ever—"

"No," Connor lied, and buried his nose back in his book.

48

"The investor sent another update," said Mr. Wi-Fi, presenting Oracle with his laptop.

Lifting the silver-mirrored aviator sunglasses from his nose, the pirate leader peered at the digital photo displayed on the laptop screen. A wash of turquoise-blue waters kissed the white sands of a palm-fringed bay, behind which rose a mist-shrouded peak.

"What island is that?"

"Mahé," replied Mr. Wi-Fi.

Oracle raised a dubious eyebrow. "There are countless islands that look the same. How can you be so certain?"

Mr. Wi-Fi right-clicked on the image, opening up its EXIF metadata file. "Because the photo has the exact geo-location embedded within it. Along with a time stamp indicating the precise moment it was taken—14:32 today."

Oracle reclined against his gold-tasseled bolster in the shaded living room and laughed. "Oh, the benefits of modern technology and the naiveté of young people. They're almost inviting us to join them!"

Reaching across to a cup on an inlaid ivory tray, he took a sip of spiced black tea. He savored the taste a moment before asking, "What other information has the investor provided?"

Sitting cross-legged on the crimson rug before his boss, Mr. Wi-Fi tugged casually at his goatee. "The *Orchid* is on a northeast bearing, headed for the Maldives. Estimated voyage time four days."

"And where are my men now?"

Mr. Wi-Fi brought up an electronic chart of the Indian Ocean on his laptop. Zooming in, he pointed to a cluster of tiny green dots visible amid a vast swath of blue.

"They're seventy-five nautical miles northwest of the target."

"Then tell Spearhead to stop playing with small fry," said Oracle, putting down his tea. "It's time to reel in the big fish."

49

Leaning against the *Orchid*'s stern rail, Connor watched Praslin Island slowly shrink toward the darkening horizon. Mahé had long since disappeared from view, and soon they'd be leaving the territorial waters of the Seychelles for the open ocean. With his cell-phone signal down to a single bar, Connor checked in with Alpha team one last time. Charley answered in two rings.

"So how are you coping solo?" she asked.

"Fine," replied Connor, not wanting to admit that he'd spent most of the afternoon evading Chloe's advances. With nothing else to do on board except read, relax and sunbathe, Chloe seemed to want to let off steam by flirting with him— a fact that hadn't gone unnoticed by her sister.

Not that Connor didn't appreciate such attention. But he knew any such lapse of judgment would finish his role as a guardian for good and bring an end to the paid-for nursing care his mum and gran so critically needed.

"Well, Luciana's on schedule to rendezvous with you in the Maldives," advised Charley. "Ling's on her way back home, but before boarding, she mentioned that you thought you'd spotted the two muggers on Praslin Island."

"I thought so, but I was wrong," admitted Connor.

"Well, there's a strong chance you may have been right."

Connor went rigid at the news. "How come?"

"The two suspects were pinged getting on a flight to Dubai the same day the Sterlings departed for their vacation. They were using false passports, so their trail went dead after that, but Dubai is a natural stopover en route to the Seychelles."

Connor tightened his grip on the phone. So his eyes *hadn't* deceived him that day.

"They seem a little persistent for muggers, and too well resourced," Charley continued. "Because they're heavies-for-hire, we can only assume someone has paid them to do a job on the Sterlings."

"Who?"

"It could be any one of Mr. Sterling's enemies. Amir's going through his threat report to see if there are any obvious links."

"Well, they've missed their opportunity here," said Connor, watching Mahé retreat into the distance.

"Unless they were responsible for the Jet-Ski incident."

Connor thought this over. "I don't see how they could have gotten on board the yacht without being noticed. Brad's run an almost constant watch since the Sterlings' arrival."

"Still, it's a possibility. If they're determined enough to follow you to the Seychelles, then they won't be far behind in the Maldives either. So stay alert."

"Will do," said Connor. "I'll contact you as soon as we reach harbor again."

"Okay," she replied. "And, Connor, be careful applying that suntan lotion."

"What?"

But Charley had already ended the call.

Connor stared at his phone, unable to believe Ling had reported that incident. Now Charley had the completely wrong idea and, judging by the tone of her voice, wasn't too happy about it. Furious with Ling, he shoved his phone into his top pocket and headed across the main deck to the salon. As he slid open the glass doors, he heard someone else on the phone.

"Anything could happen at sea. The girls are on their own. I understand your concern, Joey, but I can handle them." Amanda turned around, brushing a lock of golden hair from her eyes, and spotted Connor. "Listen, I'd better go. Ciao."

Switching off her pink diamond-studded phone, she perched herself on the edge of a leather couch. With the setting sun streaming through the window behind her, Amanda's pose was straight out of a high-class fashion shoot.

"Can I help you, Connor?" she asked, dazzling him with her smile. "I was just on the phone to my agent."

For a moment, Connor was struck dumb by her beauty. "No . . . I was simply going to make sure Chloe and Emily were okay."

"Ah, that's sweet," she said, sauntering over and ruffling his hair. "But I don't think we have anything to worry about, do you?"

Connor's eyes followed her departing figure as she strolled out the door and disappeared on the deck.

"Careful, Connor. She's a real siren."

Connor spun around to discover Brad standing at the other end of the salon, a wicked grin on his face.

"A siren?" Connor queried.

"Yeah, the femme fatales of Greek mythology. Beautiful yet dangerous creatures who'd lure unwary sailors onto the rocks with their enchanting voices and looks." He beckoned Connor over. "Speaking of danger, since Mr. Sterling's departure with Dan, we're a man down on the watch. And with Ling gone too, I definitely need you to keep an extra-sharp lookout while we're at sea."

Connor nodded. "No problem. I can take one of the shifts if you'd like."

Brad patted him on the shoulder. "Good of you to volunteer. Since you're so keen, you can do dawn duty, four till eight tomorrow morning."

Connor made a face.

"I know it's early, but ideally that slot won't draw attention to your true role. So, best get your head down while you can, tiger."

Wishing he hadn't been quite so eager, Connor headed down to his cabin on the lower deck. As he passed a door to the tender garage, he thought he heard a noise. A *clunk*. Out of curiosity, he opened the bulkhead door and peered inside. The automatic lights were already on.

"Hello? Geoff?" he called, thinking that it might be the ship's engineer.

But there was no response. On a quick inspection, he found the garage to be empty, save for the tender, the remaining Jet Ski and an array of diving gear. Yet Connor's sixth sense was tingling—a sensation he wasn't alone. Then he spotted the inflatable doughnut on the floor. It had come loose from its fixing. Connor put it back on its hook and returned to the bulkhead. Before shutting the door behind him, he took one last look around, but any feelings of being watched had vanished as quickly as they'd appeared.

50

Spearhead stood on the prow of the skiff, staring out at the darkened horizon. The sun had yet to make its mark in the predawn sky, and the stars still glimmered overhead. The tiny boat, no more than a piece of flotsam in the vast expanse of the Indian Ocean, rocked and rolled, but Spearhead rode the waves with a fisherman's ease.

"See anything yet?" Big Mouth called over the steady rumble of his skiff's outboard motor.

Spearhead didn't bother replying. He'd let them know when it was time.

They'd sighted the *Orchid* the previous day and trailed their prey through the night. It had been easy to follow the *Orchid*'s navigation lights, but nobody aboard the yacht would have been able to detect their small flotilla of unlit skiffs.

"We've been shadowing them for *hours*," moaned Juggs,

his lanky body laid out across a wooden seat, oversized feet dangling over the water. "If we were in the Gulf of Aden, a hundred cargo ships would have passed us by now. Easy pickings."

"I agree," yawned Big Mouth, standing up and urinating over the side. "Why chase a dolphin when we can land a whale?"

"Oracle foresaw this bounty," muttered a pirate as he tried to sleep beneath a red headscarf. "When has he ever been wrong?"

Having relieved himself, Big Mouth pulled up his shorts. "I just don't understand why we couldn't attack when we first found the *Orchid*."

"Because," Spearhead explained with irritation, "we need to hunt like sharks—attack when least expected, when the prey is least ready to fight back."

His keen eyes spotted the pinpoint flash of light on the horizon. There were three more bursts in quick succession.

"That's our signal," he announced, and raised his assault rifle in the air to alert the rest of the gang.

The pirates in the other skiffs pulled aside the nets covering their weapons. AK-47s were ripped from their plastic wrappings and magazines rammed home. The harsh *click* and *clack* of assault rifles being primed and loaded punctured the air above the growl of outboard motors.

After several days of enforced idleness, there was an urgency to the pirates' actions, all the men eager to sink their teeth into some violence.

Big Mouth pried open the wooden box containing his RPG. Loading a rocket into the launcher, he lifted it to his lips and kissed the tip.

"Time to earn your keep!" he said, resting the mighty weapon in his lap.

Spearhead checked his AK-47 one final time, ensuring the action was smooth. He didn't want any jams during the assault. He'd known of too many incidents when salt water had corroded older weapons and left a pirate high and dry in the middle of an attack.

Twirling his finger in the air and pointing ahead, Spearhead signaled for the hijack to commence. The powerful outboards roared and the skiffs accelerated away, charging through the waves like a pack of killer whales in pursuit of their prey.

51

Connor yawned and looked at his watch—5:30 a.m.

Zipping up his jacket to fend off the chilly sea breeze, he paced the top deck. Through the night-vision lenses of his sunglasses, the stars appeared overly bright in the sky, like theater spotlights, and the sea shimmered as if awash with mercury.

Raising the binoculars to his eyes, he performed another sweep of the horizon. So far the only other vessels he'd sighted were a fishing trawler and the long, low profile of an oil tanker. Both had glided by in distant silence, no more than ghosts in the night.

Connor stifled another yawn. His lookout duty was progressing with painful slowness. He couldn't believe that he still had another two and a half hours to go, but at least the sun would be up soon. The faintest of glows was now visible to the east, pushing back the curtain of night.

As he completed his sweep, his eye caught a glint of

something directly to the *Orchid's* stern. Adjusting the focus on his binoculars, he zoomed in on the point near the horizon, but the roll of the yacht made it hard to keep the image steady.

Was that a boat? A wave? Or just another whale?

He'd spotted a small pod of humpback whales within the first ten minutes of his watch. The spray from their blowholes had looked like fountains of silver through his night-vision glasses. It was his first encounter with these magnificent creatures, and he'd been spellbound by their appearance. Then the whales had dived deep and he'd lost them among the waves.

It seemed this was the case again. He scanned the ocean once more but saw nothing. Then his attention was grabbed by the faint reflection of a flashing light from the main deck below. He leaned over the rail, but couldn't detect the source.

Descending two flights of steps, he made his way to the starboard side and discovered Emily standing beside the rail.

"Morning," he said.

She snapped her head around in surprise, but quickly recovered and greeted him with a wry smile. "Barely," she replied.

"Did you see a flashing light?"

Emily shook her head. "Only just got here. Maybe it was from the salon as I walked through?"

Connor frowned. "Possibly, but the beam seemed more

focused than that." He looked up and down the deck, but all was dark.

Emily stared at him, then waved a hand in front of his face. "Can you even see? Why are you wearing sunglasses at night?"

"Oh, these." Connor flipped them back off his head. He wasn't sure if Amir wanted the secrets of his gear revealed, so he replied, "They're part of the standard-issue Guardian uniform. Sometimes I forget I'm wearing them."

"Well, you're missing out on the sunrise," said Emily, turning to the rail and admiring the expanding halo of red fire on the horizon.

Connor joined her. "Is that why you're up so early?"

"Not really. I was finding it hard to sleep." She glanced timidly at him. "Nightmares."

Connor nodded, but didn't press any further. He could only imagine what horrors she dreamed of after her kidnapping ordeal.

The sun continued its ascent, heralding another glorious day at sea.

"I'm feeling a little hungry," Emily announced. "Chef usually leaves some snacks in the galley. Can I get you anything?"

Having risen so early, Connor suddenly realized that he was ravenous. "That would be great. I'd kill for an orange juice and a piece of toast."

"No need to go that far!" Emily laughed. "I'll see what I can find."

She headed inside, leaving Connor alone with the sunrise. Its first golden rays graced the ocean, streaking the tops of the waves a deep molten orange. Lulled by the view, Connor almost drifted into Code White ... but was snapped back to full alert by the glimpse of several dark shapes on the horizon.

52

Connor hammered on Brad's cabin door. He peered out, bleary eyed. "What's up?"

Connor told him what he'd seen—or at least what he thought he'd seen. The shapes had been so small and distant that he couldn't be absolutely certain—and he'd soon lost sight of them amid the crests of the ocean waves.

"Give me a minute." Brad closed the door and then emerged, dressed.

They made their way to the upper deck. Connor pointed in the direction he'd spotted the suspect boats. Brad borrowed Connor's binoculars and swept the horizon.

"I don't see anything. Let's check the radar," he said, heading for the bridge.

Captain Locke had just come on duty. "Are you sure about what you saw, Brad?" he asked, glancing at the radar screen, which showed nothing within eight nautical miles of the *Orchid*.

"Well, I didn't spot them," Brad admitted. "Connor did. He was on watch."

Chief Officer Fielding, who had the wheel, glared at Brad in astonishment. "This boy was on *watch*? What were you thinking?"

"Connor is more than capable of—"

"Oh, don't bother," he cut in, shooting Connor a withering glare. "I can't believe you gave the responsibility of a watch shift to a *boy*. That's a serious breach of security protoc—"

"Pardon for interrupting," said the Second Officer, "but I'm picking up an unidentified vessel fast approaching our stern."

Captain Locke rose from his chair and studied the radar screen again. A green dot was now traversing the monitor on a direct course for the *Orchid*. Then several more blips appeared, all converging rapidly on the center. A second later, the blips were gone.

"Whoever they are, they're in our radar shadow," said Captain Locke, his expression hardening. "Get me a visual confirmation."

Brad ran back outside onto the upper deck, Connor close on his heels. The sun was now fully up, a burning ball of red in the dawn sky. They scanned the ocean to the *Orchid*'s stern. Half a mile directly south, five skiffs loaded with men surged across the waves.

Brad sprinted back to the captain. "Five skiffs. Pirates, by the looks of it."

"How long to contact?" asked Captain Locke.

"Less than five minutes," replied the second officer.

Captain Locke leaned upon the radar terminal, his jaw set firm. "If their approach is anything to go by, they mean business. Chief Officer, full speed ahead," he commanded.

Chief Officer Fielding drove the throttle home. From deep within the bowels of the *Orchid*, a mighty rumble shook the super-yacht as the twin diesel engines were pushed to their max.

The captain picked up the yacht's speaker mic. "Calling all crew. Calling all crew. This is the captain speaking. We have a Red Alert. I repeat, a Red Alert. All hands to the bridge."

Brad turned to Connor. "Get Emily and Chloe to the citadel."

Without needing to be told twice, Connor turned for the door as Geoff burst onto the bridge.

"What's going on, Captain?" said the engineer, frowning with deep concern when he saw the rev counter in the red zone. "The engines won't keep this up for long."

"Pirates," Captain Locke explained. "Attempting to hijack us."

"They're still gaining," announced the chief officer, nodding toward the radar where a swarm of green blips reappeared momentarily.

Captain Locke grimaced. "Prepare to send a distress call."

Realizing there wasn't much time, Connor headed below

deck to look for Emily in the galley. As he raced from the bridge and down the steps, he caught a glimpse of the skiffs cutting like sharks' fins through the waves. He could make out the pirates, bristling with weaponry. This was the nightmare scenario they'd planned for—yet prayed would never happen.

Dashing along a corridor and into the sleek white galley, Connor found Emily by the fridge pouring out a glass of fresh orange juice.

"I've got your breakfast," she said, smiling at him as she put the glass on a tray, along with a plate of buttered toast.

"No time for that." Grabbing her arm, he pulled her out of the galley and hustled her over to the stairwell.

"Hey! What's the problem?" she cried.

"Pirates. We don't have long before—" The *Orchid* slammed hard against the swell. The impact was bone shattering. Emily lost her footing, and Connor barely kept her from tumbling down the stairs.

"Keep hold of the rail," he urged as they descended the staircase to the lower deck.

Rushing along the corridor to Chloe's room, they could see the walls vibrating from the thrum of the engines. Connor hammered on the door. "Chloe! Chloe! Open up!"

"What is it?" came a sleepy reply.

With no time for discretion, he threw open the door. She sat bolt upright, clutching the bedding around her. "Sorry, but this is an emergency. Grab some clothes. We need to get you to the citadel fast."

"Citadel?" said Chloe, staring at him wide eyed and confounded.

"Safe room," explained Connor. "We're under attack from pirates. Now hurry."

Too stunned and terrified to protest, she bundled some clothes into her arms and allowed herself to be herded into the corridor. Connor pushed the two sisters along and up the stairs. At the bulkhead to the crew's quarters, they met Amanda being escorted by Brad.

"Stay in there until I give the all clear. Understood?" said Brad.

Amanda nodded mutely, her angelic features pale with shock. Connor ushered Chloe and Emily in after her, then turned to follow Brad.

"Where are you going?" Chloe cried, a look of abandonment on her face.

Connor hoped his nerves didn't show as he replied, "To fight off the pirates."

53

Standing on the main deck, Connor clutched the rail, the wind whipping at his face and hair. Below him, the water rushed past like a surging torrent and the *Orchid* left a huge foamy wake in her trail. But fast as she was, the pirates doggedly closed the distance: 1,000 feet . . . 800 feet . . . 600 feet . . .

"Those are *powerful* engines," remarked Brad. "They've got to be doing over thirty knots."

He spoke into the two-way radio. "Captain, you need to fishtail."

There was a crackle of static. *"We'll lose speed,"* came the reply.

Brad pressed the Transmit button. "We won't outrun them in a straight sprint. We need to make it difficult to board."

"Understood."

A second later, the *Orchid* lurched off course, veering hard to port. Connor gripped the rail, then was thrown against the chrome bar as she cut back toward starboard. Each switch sent a heavy wash in the pirates' direction. The skiffs rode them like bucking broncos, seawater breaking over their bows and sending spray high into the air. The pirates clung to their seats, in danger of being tossed from their craft. But, like a waterborne wolf pack, the skiffs hounded the *Orchid* on all sides. As one fell back, another took its place.

Connor's mouth became dry, a mix of adrenaline and fear. He licked his lips, but tasted only salt water. He could feel his heart pounding and imagined this to be like the blind rush of panic a fox felt during a hunt.

A skiff came level with the *Orchid*'s port side. A pirate waved an AK-47 for them to slow down.

"He's got to be joking," said Brad, turning to Connor. "Do you have the flares ready? Looks like we'll be needing them sooner rather than later."

Connor nodded and primed a flare gun. The other deckhands were stationed around the boat, ready to fend off any attempt to board.

Seeing that their prey had no intention of stopping, the pirate leveled his AK-47 and fired indiscriminately at the *Orchid*. Connor ducked, sheltering behind the gunwale as the deadly *zing* of bullets whizzed over their heads.

"They're trying to kill us!" cried Jordan, cowering on the deck farther down.

"Warning shots," Brad replied. "To scare us."

"Well, it's working!"

Taking the flare gun from Connor, Brad waited for a break in the hail of bullets, then stood up and fired back at the skiff. A red blaze zoomed through the air. The pirate dived into his boat as the flare streaked across his bow, almost knocking him into the sea. But this single attack didn't deter him. He immediately rose and retaliated with another burst of gunfire. Bullets ripped into the fiberglass hull. The *Orchid's* crew cringed in terror behind the gunwales, their hands covering their heads.

The *Orchid* swung hard to port, forcing the attacking skiff to back off.

However, another skiff immediately came up on her starboard side. Brad and Connor rushed across. A pirate crouched in the skiff's bow; on his shoulder was the long drainpipe-like barrel of a rocket launcher. Connor flashed back to the shaky video from Alpha team's briefing and felt a chill run through him . . . This time *he* was a part of it.

Brad snatched up his radio. "Captain, skiff to starboard. Ram them!"

"*Too risky.*"

"They have an RPG!"

The skiff had pulled level with the bridge and the pirate was taking aim.

"I see it," replied the captain. *"Oh my—"*

His transmission cut off as the pirate launched the rocket. It scorched through the air, blazing a trail across the open water. Connor watched in wide-eyed horror as the ball of hellfire rocketed straight toward them.

To be continued . . .

Turn the Page for a Sneak Peek at

Book 4: Ransom

The buzzing woke Amir. He yawned and glanced at his watch: 03:30.

Why had he set his alarm for so early?

As he rubbed the sleep from his eyes, the alarm continued its incessant buzzing. He reached over to switch it off and promptly fell to the floor. Dazed, Amir looked around the darkened briefing room and at his upturned chair. Of course, he wasn't in bed. He was on night duty, supposedly monitoring Operation Gemini.

The buzzing grew more urgent, and Amir scrambled up to his desk. On the glowing computer screen a Red Alert icon was flashing. Clicking on the pulsing box, he stared at the few stark lines of text, then grabbed his phone.

"What is it, Amir?" Charley answered drowsily.

"Distress call from the *Orchid*."

There was a moment's silence as the words sank in. Then she replied, "I'll be right down," her voice sharp and alert.

A short while later, Charley wheeled herself through the door, wearing a T-shirt and sweatpants.

"What information do we have?"

Amir nodded to his computer screen. "The *Orchid* sent out a DSC distress signal at 0625 hours, Seychelles local time. It gave her position as two hundred and forty nautical miles east-northeast of Mahé."

"Do we know the actual problem?"

Amir swallowed anxiously. "Pirates."

Charley looked at him. "Seems like you've lost your bet with Ling," she said, her tone bereft of humor. "Any communication from Connor?"

Amir shook his head. "The distress signal was picked up by the Seychelles Maritime Rescue and Coordination Center. Since the *Orchid*'s out of range for VHF radio and cell phones, a satellite call is the only possible option. But there's no mention of it in this report."

Charley picked up the phone. "I'll contact the Seychelles coast guard for an update. In the meantime, wake Colonel Black, then see if you can get through to Connor via your SOS app."

ACKNOWLEDGMENTS

This is Connor's second assignment and it's even tougher than the first. I can tell you, the writing process doesn't get any easier for me either. The bar to entertain, surprise and thrill the reader is set higher each time. That's why I continue to rely on so many people to ensure I deliver the best story I can. So I'd like to thank the following people, who have supported me from start to finish:

My long-suffering wife, Sarah, who has to manage the ebbs and flows of elation and despair that I experience when writing. My two wonderful sons, Zach and Leo, you are a constant inspiration for me. My mum and dad, who diligently help proofread all my drafts. Sue and Simon for helping with the boys and keeping our garden looking lovely. Steve and Sam for taking the boys swimming, and Karen and Rob for being such wonderful friends.

Charlie Viney, my agent, who has my best interests at heart all the time. Clemmie Gaisman and Nicky Kennedy at ILA. Pippa Le Quesne for her insightful advice.

My team of loyal editors: Brian Geffen at Philomel Books, who has made this edition even more explosive; Tig Wallace at Puffin for his steady hand on the tiller; and Wendy Shakespeare at Puffin for her ever watchful copy-editing eye!

A special thanks must go to Abdilahi Nur and his mother for checking the Somali translation. *Mahadsanid.*

Trevor Wilson and Shelley Lee at Authors Abroad for all their diligent work in organizing my book tours around the world.

And all my good friends for their encouragement and support, including but not exclusive to Geoff and Lucy, Matt, Charlie, Jackie and Russell, the members of the HGC (Dan, Siggy, Larry, Dean, Giles), my cousin Laura and the Dyson clan (especially my goddaughter Lulu!).

Stay safe.
Chris

Any fans can keep in touch with me via my YouTube channel ChrisBradfordAuthor or my website www.chrisbradford.co.uk